The Mayan Mystery

Books in the Choice Adventures series

The Mayan Mystery

Kent Keller

Tyndale House Publishers, Inc.
Wheaton, Illinois

Library of Congress Cataloging-in-Publication Data

Keller, Kent.
  The Mayan mystery / Kent Keller.
    p.   cm. — (Choice adventures ; #14)
  Summary: The reader's choices determine the course of the adventures of a group of junior high boys on a short-term missions project to the Yucatán.
    ISBN 0-8423-5132-9
  1. Plot-your-own stories.   [1. Christian life—Fiction.   2. Adventure and adventurers—Fiction.   3. Yucatán (Mexico : State)—Fiction.   4. Plot-your-own stories.]   I. Title.   II. Series.
PZ7.K281345May   1994
[Fic]—dc20   93-48838

Printed in the United States of America

99 98 97 96 95 94
 7   6   5   4   3   2   1

For Christian and Andrew—two of the best choices and greatest adventures of my life

Man, it's hot down here," said Chris. "I didn't think any place in the world could be hotter than Millersburg in July, but Mérida is." Chris and Willy and Sam—part of a group of kids called the Ringers—were walking from the plane to the airport terminal in Mérida, Mexico. "I sure hope it's air-conditioned in there."

"Don't count on it," Sam said. "I haven't been in Mérida before, but if it's like the rest of Mexico, you can forget your *aire acondicionado,* señor." Sam laughed at the pained expressions on Chris's and Willy's faces. "You Americanos are so spoiled!" The truth was, Samuel Ramirez was as American as any of the kids on this mission trip, but he liked to act as though he wasn't.

Sam, Willy Washington, and Chris Martin were the only three of the Ringers who had stuck with the idea of going on this mission trip to Mexico's Yucatán Peninsula. Several of the other Ringers had wanted to go but had backed out for various reasons. But Jessica Andrews, Chris's next-door neighbor, had surprised them all by coming along. She was shy by nature and not officially part of the Ringers gang, so when she told the others she wanted to go, they were surprised and wondered if it was a good idea.

But here she was, along with Sam, Willy, Chris, and twenty-five other people from other churches in the Washington, D.C., area, walking across the tarmac of the

Mérida airport in the saunalike heat of late July. Like the others, she was hoping the terminal would be air-conditioned, but a few steps inside toward the baggage claim area told them that it was not to be. The four kids from Millersburg stood together, watching the empty luggage carousel whine past them, waiting for their bags to appear. It was exciting and scary at the same time to be standing there in this strange new place, listening to the sounds of people speaking Spanish all around them. As they waited, they remembered that night several months before, when they first heard about the chance to spend two weeks on a mission trip to the Yucatán Peninsula.

"What are you doing this summer?" Jeff Ellers, the youth director from nearby Fairfax Congregational Church, asked them. The Ringers and the other kids at Capitol Community Church in Millersburg listened more attentively than usual as Jeff issued a challenge to them. "You can sit around here, bored as usual, watching TV, doing the same old things, or you can join a bunch of us on an adventure that could change your life and the lives of a lot of other people. We're going to spend two weeks serving the Lord in the village of San Felipe down on the Yucatán Peninsula."

Chris stuck up his hand, and Jeff nodded at him. "Where is this 'You-can-tan' peninsula?"

Sam leaped to his feet, pretending to be shocked and saying with a very obvious accent, "How *could* you! After all I've tried to teach you about my people, *ai-yai-yai*, señor Krees. The Yucatán peneensula ees in *Meh-hee-koe,* the country ees shaped like a faat, backwards *J,* and the

Yucatán makes up the tip of the hook. And yes, 'you-can-tan' there, too."

Jeff chuckled and then went on, "We sure need people like you, Sam, who can speak the language, to help us with this trip. And if we have to put up with your friends . . . well, that would be great! But listen, it's going to be hot . . . and hard . . . and it will push you to the limit. It's not for everybody. But if you're serious about serving God and his people, this will be a tremendous opportunity for you. Think about it—the same old summer routine . . . or an adventure that could change your life. Which would you rather do?"

Adventure—that word was like putting a match to a fuse for Willy, Chris, and Sam. Jessica had her own reasons for wanting to go. So, while other kids who also said they would go had dropped out for various reasons, these four had stuck with it, raised the money, and were now standing in the Mérida airport.

Sam had convinced his cousin Gonzalo Alvarez, who lived in Miami, to come along as well, and he was supposed to meet them here in the Mérida airport as soon as they cleared immigration. Sam hoped he would be able to find Gonzalo, or "Gonzo," as he preferred to be called.

At that moment the brightly colored duffel bags began making their way around the track, and the kids grabbed them and headed for the customs counters. After a routine search of their bags, they were sent through tinted glass doors and found themselves outside again, this time in front of the airport. The heat hit them like a blast furnace again, and the intense Yucatán sun made them all whip out their sunglasses.

4

"Now I know why we call it You-can-tan . . . ," mumbled someone.

"Check out the military dudes over there," Willy said to the others. "I wonder why they all need to be armed like that just to stand in front of an airport." They all turned to get a better look at the soldiers standing about twenty feet away from them. The sight of these very serious-looking young men with M-16s was a little unsettling. Before the Ringers' stares made them too obvious, however, they were distracted by a noise right behind them. They turned around just in time to see Sam's orange duffel bag disappearing around a corner.

"Hey! My bag!" Sam yelled.

CHOICE ⇒

If the kids take off after Sam's bag themselves, turn to page 36.

If Sam pursues the bag alone, turn to page 89.

Jess was walking over to the trailer for tools when she realized that Sam and Gonzo were no longer with her. They were whispering some distance away from her. It seemed as if they were trying to decide something.

She began to get suspicious. . . .

CHOICE➡

If she decides to say something to the boys, turn to page 135.

If she lets it go, turn to page 70.

6

Jeff and the Ringers made it back to the ruins at Tulum in record time. They split into three teams and began to look for Danny. They had to work fast because they were rapidly running out of daylight.

It didn't take the group long to cover the entire ancient city—small compared to many other ruins. They ran to the top of the biggest structures, looked inside the ones that could be looked into, and poked around behind the ones that were large enough to hide someone from view.

No Danny.

The team reassembled just inside the front entrance, catching their breath and looking around at the ruins, now casting long shadows in the late-afternoon sun.

"What now?" Chris asked.

"Why don't we ask the vendors and the shopkeepers out front if any of them have seen him?" Matt suggested.

"Good idea," Jeff agreed.

They exited through the front gate and began asking the locals if they had seen anyone matching Danny's description. Carlos found a man who remembered seeing someone like that—headed south, down the highway.

"Great," breathed Jeff. His worst fears were coming true. It was almost sunset, and a runaway American teenager was roaming around the Yucatán Peninsula. *Lord,*

he prayed silently, *please watch over that boy and keep
him safe!*

"Let's load up and head south," said Jeff, trying not to
sound worried.

As they drove, the group used what little light they
had left to scan the road for any sign of a slender American
teenager with long hair and his ever-present denim jacket.
Their hopes of finding Danny were sinking with the sun.

Jessica saw him first. "There he is!" she blurted, so loudly
that it startled everyone.

Danny was walking along the left side of the road,
away from the highway. They couldn't see his face, but
there was no doubt it was him: denim jacket, long hair,
slender build. Jeff wasted no time pulling the van up in
front of him, blocking his path. The whole gang spilled out
of the vehicle.

"Danny," Jeff said, trying not to sound as angry as he
really felt. "You want to tell me what you're doing out
here?"

Danny stared at the ground, seemingly unaware of the
group that had now gathered behind Jeff. He sank his teeth
into his lip, fumbling for words. Jeff couldn't tell whether
he looked sad, lonely, or frightened.

Finally Danny spoke.

"Just let me go, Jeff," he said, his voice barely more
than a whisper. "Please, just let me go . . . just let me
disappear. It'll be better for everyone. Please, Jeff . . ." His
voice trailed off, and he stared again at his feet.

"Why, Danny? What's so terrible that would make you
want to run off like this out here in the middle of nowhere?

8

You know I can't let you do this. Everyone has been worried sick about you. You want to start explaining what this is all about?" Jeff's tone softened a little as he looked at this very unhappy young man.

"You wouldn't understand, man. None of you would," Danny said, looking at the others for the first time. "You've all got good homes, parents that love you, or at least don't hate you, and you've got friends. You can't understand what I'm going through."

"Is that what this is about, Danny?" Matt spoke for the first time. "Things at home are bad, so you thought you'd make a break for it down here?"

Danny was silent.

"OK," Jeff said. "Danny's got some explaining to do. Right now I think we need to get going back to San Felipe. It's getting late, and everyone is going to be worrying about us. Let's load up. We'll deal with this when we get back."

With that, the team piled into the van again to begin the long, quiet ride to San Felipe. Most of the kids slept, Jeff drove, and Danny stared out at the dark countryside, wondering what would happen next.

They arrived back at the dorm at Príncipe de Paz a little after midnight. Most of the kids in the van had to be awakened when they pulled up to the dorm. As Matt helped them get their bearings and herded them toward their rooms, Jeff explained to the other adults—Bob, Beth, and Mrs. Jordan—what had happened.

"I told him we wouldn't try to make any decisions about what to do with him tonight," Jeff said. "He knows he's blown it big-time and that we are all going to have to talk about what to do with him. The big question is, Do we send him home at his mother's expense or not?"

Beth started to offer her opinion, but Jeff held up his hand. "Please, guys, let's not get into it tonight. I'm wiped out, and I'm sure you must be, too. Let's get some sleep and meet in the morning."

"I think that's wise, Jeff," Bob offered. They all said good night and hit the sack.

The next morning came brutally early to the ones who had helped find Danny and gotten in so late. Immediately after breakfast, Jeff called all the adults together to discuss Danny's situation. He also asked Chris and Willy to be there. There was no question that Danny needed to be disciplined; the only question was how.

It was a difficult problem. Some were concerned about Danny's problems at home and didn't think it would do any good to send him back. Others felt that Danny needed to obey the rules just like everybody else did and that it wouldn't be fair to make an exception for him.

Finally, everyone looked back to Jeff. It was his decision to make.

CHOICE ⇒

If Jeff sends Danny home, turn to page 56.

If he gives Danny another chance, turn to page 41.

Willy, Chris, and Danny volunteered for one of the jobs. At Bob's direction, they went and got a shovel and some hand tools from the tool trailer and met Bob on the far side of the cement slab. On the ground he had marked a rectangular shape in the dirt.

"We planning to bury those who don't make it?" asked Danny, much to his partners' surprise. When Danny relaxed, he had a good sense of humor.

Bob chuckled. "Not exactly. But I will tell you that your job is very important, and the longer you take, the more impatient people you may discover. Your mission is to dig and build the *baño*. We would call it an outhouse."

"We're building an outhouse for the church?" asked Danny.

"I'm not sure if the church will use it or not," answered Bob, "but I'm pretty sure we're gonna need one while we're working here—'specially if any of us drink the unfiltered water!"

The boys got lots of encouragement from the other workers as they dug. The ground was hard red clay. It was easy for making the holes straight and even, but it was stiff and heavy.

Under the direction of Juan, they took turns digging while the other two worked on building the walls and doors. Several hours and many blisters later, their clothes had all taken on the red color of the soil. At last they pounded the walls together and put on the roof—they had constructed an outhouse. But that wasn't the only thing they had built that day. Willy, Chris, and Danny had built a friendship.

Funny how shoveling, hammering, and joking around together helps strangers become friends.

THE END

You don't have to end here! This was only one of the building projects or adventures on the trip. If you think the Ringers are ready for a break from their work, turn to page 108 to find out where they went on their day off.

Or, for other adventures, turn back to the beginning and make different choices along the way.

12

Following two apparent thieves outside where there was room to run was one thing; going inside an ancient pyramid where there was . . . *what?* . . . was another.

"I don't know, man," Willy said. "Those guys could have guns! Out here we've got a chance to get away if we need to. If we go in there and get in a jam, who would know? I say we go for help."

"Yeah, you're right," Chris agreed. Actually, he was quite relieved Willy had suggested they go for help. He would have gone inside the pyramid rather than look chicken, but he didn't really want to.

Of course, there was the matter of explaining to the security guards or the police or *whomever* exactly what they had been doing sneaking around out there while the show was going on. They were obviously not supposed to be out there. But they decided to tell the truth and face the consequences, whatever they were.

The lights were still on another part of the ancient city, so the boys decided to cut back to the entrance, taking the shortest possible route. And if they got caught, well . . . they were looking for a security guard anyway.

They also needed somebody to translate for them. Coming back around to where they had left the path before, they found the place where the group was still sitting, listening to the last part of the show. Jeff heard them coming and turned around and motioned them over to him.

"Where have you guys *been?*"

"No time to explain right now, Jeff—but would you and Sam and Gonzo come with us, *quick?*" Chris's face showed he was serious; Jeff leaned over and waved for Sam and Gonzo to come with them.

Hurrying back to the entrance, Willy explained in sketchy detail what had happened: going to look for Carlos, seeing the two suspicious-looking guys, following them, seeing them cut the lock and disappear into El Castillo. "OK, guys," Jeff responded. "We're going to get the guards and see what this is all about. But when we're done, you two"—he pointed at Willy and Chris—"and I are going to have a little chat."

"Yes sir," said Chris.

They found two security guards at the front gate. Sam hurriedly explained what Chris and Willy had seen. The guards looked quizzically at the two boys, then one got on his walkie-talkie and made a quick transmission. He told Sam to have Chris and Willy stay with him and for the others to follow. Two policemen pulled up in their car, jumped out, and ran over to join them. The guard hurriedly explained what had happened, and the officers led the way out toward El Castillo.

Having no need for staying out of sight as the others had, they made the shortest approach toward the door leading into the inner part of the pyramid. All four officers carried long flashlights and nightsticks, and the policemen had their pistols unfastened as well. When they got within twenty yards of the door, they told Jeff and the kids to stay back out of the way, and they crept up to the doorway.

Before they could get there, the door opened and two figures emerged, one carrying a medium-sized duffel bag. All four officers trained their flashlights on them instantly, and the lead policemen yelled out, *"Alto!"* ("Stop!")

Two surprised thieves looked up in disbelief at the flashlights blinding them. Unable to see, they set the bag down and put their hands in the air. The policeman told them to lie down and extend their arms, which they did. As soon as they were both face down on the ground, the officers handcuffed them and pulled them roughly to their feet.

"Let's see what you have in the bag," he growled in Spanish.

The duffel bag held four priceless artifacts they had taken from an inner chamber. Holstering their guns, the policemen led the men back to the entrance and then into their waiting patrol car.

Before leaving, however, they questioned Willy and Chris (with Sam interpreting), lecturing them sternly about the foolishness of what they had done. They also thanked them for helping them nail a couple of would-be thieves. Many ancient ruin sites had been vandalized by men like them, and many priceless relics had disappeared.

Before they rejoined the others, however, Jeff had a heart-to-heart talk with Chris and Willy. He told them that for running off without permission they would have to do some kind of "community service" for the others when they got back.

THE END

16

The second Sunday was the high point of the whole trip. Everything else they had done—all the hot, sweaty days on the concrete slab, the Bible school, everything—was done in preparation for this day. Sunday was the day they would dedicate the new building.

All the kids were involved in the dedication ceremony. Pastor Julio led the service, but he had asked the group to participate, too. Matt had taught the kids a couple of songs, even one in Spanish. Cheryl had surprised them all with such a beautiful voice that Matt asked her to sing a solo.

After an opening greeting from Julio, Jeff had offered a prayer in English, followed by Sam praying in Spanish. Most of the service went that way, alternating between English and Spanish. Then the kids sang several choruses, and Cheryl sang her solo. The Mexican congregation clapped loudly.

After Scripture readings, Jeff invited the kids to come up and speak about what the trip had meant to them. As Gonzo translated, three of the kids, including Willy, told the Mexican congregation how much they had learned from their time in the Yucatán. Each speaker was met with loud applause and a mixture of amens and hallelujahs.

When the kids had finished speaking, Julio asked if anyone from his congregation would like to talk about what this group's efforts had meant to them. Two of the men and one older woman quickly stood up and took turns telling the group how much they appreciated their work. Sam translated.

When they sat down, Julio looked out at his flock and said, "Anyone else?" After a brief silence, a woman stood up at the very back of the new building. She was holding a baby.

"I have not been a part of this church," señora Garcia said in a hesitant tone. "I wasn't really interested when this group came to San Felipe to work on this building. I was more concerned about many other things, especially my sick baby.

"One morning three of the young people came to my home to tell me about the project and about the church. One of them, Yessica, saw my little Miguel and asked about him. I told her he was very sick and would die soon. She and the others took my baby to a doctor in Mérida. They saved his life. He is here with me this morning because of these young people. And we are here in this church because of their faith in Christ. I thank them, and I thank you all. May God bless you for what you have done."

Sam was so choked up he could barely translate her words.

"Praise God for what he has done for you and your husband and your baby," Julio said passionately. "Would anyone else like to say anything?"

Carlos stepped to the front. *"Buenos días, hermanos y hermanas.* Good morning, brothers and sisters." He was the only speaker who could address both groups in their own language. "My name is Carlos Celiz. Most of you know me and know my story, about how I came to live with Pastor Julio and Rosa. Most of you also know that the old woman who brought me to them told them that I was a descendant of the great Mayan king, Kukulcán himself."

Many in the Mexican congregation nodded their heads as Carlos spoke. They held him in high esteem and had great affection for him.

"For most of my life I considered my heritage the source of my importance—that I was Carlos Celiz, adopted son of Julio Celiz and descendant of the great king Kukulcán. But in spite of this, I found that my heritage did not satisfy me. It was not enough to know my past. I needed to know why *I* was put here on this earth, in this village of San Felipe.

"Two years ago, I discovered the answer. It came to me one day while I was reading the Bible and praying. My significance lies not in who my father is, or who my ancestor was, but in who I am in Christ. He doesn't care if I am the son of a king or an orphan; in my case, I am both. He loves me anyway and wants me to learn to love him. He sent his Son, Jesus, to die on a cross so that I could be forgiven of my sins. On that day two years ago, I prayed to receive Christ as my personal Savior. He paid for my sins on the cross, and I received forgiveness and eternal life."

Carlos's words were received by lots of amens, alleluias, and nodding heads.

"Our people know—and it is a source of shame for us—that our ancestors, in spite of their great accomplishments, also practiced human sacrifice. The Well of Sacrifice at Chichén Itzá alone claimed hundreds or maybe even thousands of victims. In Jesus we have an innocent one who was willing to be put to death *in our place* in order that we could know the one true God who loves us.

"My brothers and sisters, this church exists to tell people about Jesus Christ. This building has been built to give us a place to come together and worship God and to tell others of the new life we have in him. If you do not have his new life in you, invite Jesus Christ to come into your life now."

Danny had been sitting through the entire service with an emotional tug-of-war going on inside him. He was not the kind who got up in front of people and made speeches; nor was he inclined to bare his soul in front of that many strangers. And yet something had been happening in his heart on this trip. . . .

Part of him wanted to stand up and say something, but he was nervous and afraid. He knew that if he was ever going to say something, it was now or never.

CHOICE

If Danny speaks up, turn to page 139.

If he says nothing, turn to page 130.

Carlos, Jessica, and Chris had no problem going to the appropriate homes and getting the parents' (mostly mothers') interest because Carlos knew *everyone* in San Felipe. All the families they spoke with were kind, inviting the teenagers in and offering them something to drink, listening politely. Almost all expressed interest in having their children participate in the Bible school. As Beth had expected, Jess and Chris drew lots of attention, and Carlos spent most of his time interpreting back and forth between the Mexican hosts and the American guests.

Their visit to one home turned out to be unforgettable. They were invited in, and, like all the others, the woman of the house offered them chairs and something to drink. They gratefully sat down, but politely declined the drinks.

After sitting and talking with this woman for several minutes, Carlos began to answer the usual questions about the American kids—where they were from and why they were there. Since Chris and Jess couldn't answer the woman's questions, they were getting bored. Jessica's eyes roamed around the inside of the hut, taking in the simple furniture and the few items of decoration on the walls. Just then a tiny movement caught her eye.

In the corner of the room was what looked like a bundle of rags wrapped around a small object. Had she not seen the small movement, Jess would have overlooked it. She fixed her gaze on it with curiosity and a little fear.

It twitched again.

"Chris," Jess whispered. "What is that?"

"What's what?" Chris hadn't noticed anything.

"Right there." Jess nodded, not wanting to seem too obvious or rude.

Chris followed her nod and saw the bundle of rags. He stared at it for a moment and was about to conclude that it was simply that—rags—when the bundle moved again.

Then it whimpered.

Carlos and the woman stopped their conversation and turned to look at the bundle. The woman's face, which had seemed sad and older than it should have, grew even sadder. She blinked and looked from the bundle to Jessica and Chris and then sadly back to the bundle. Then she spoke to Carlos.

"That is my baby," she said in Spanish. "He is very sick. My husband says he will die soon." She paused. "We have lost two other babies the same way. They just get sick, stop nursing, and soon they die. He will die too." She paused again, this time with tears in her eyes.

"I pray to God to heal my baby, but I don't have hope. My other babies died, and many, many other babies born in San Felipe die this way, too." With that, she wiped her eyes and was silent.

Carlos, Jess, and Chris did not know what to do. Beth's instructions hadn't covered anything quite like this.

Jessica was overwhelmed by the sadness and heartbreak they were witnessing.

22

Suddenly she made up her mind. She mumbled an excuse me for Carlos to translate and hurried out of the hut. She began to run back in the direction of the work site. She wasn't sure why she was running, and she didn't care about the heat or the unfamiliar surroundings.

She ran all the way back to the site where the rest of the group was still working, laying the first courses of blocks for the walls. One of the other girls saw her coming and called Beth over to see what was happening. Jess ran straight into Beth's sweaty arms and burst into tears.

"Beth . . . Beth . . . my God . . . a baby . . ." That was all she could manage to choke out.

Turn to page 103.

Come on!" hissed Willy, and before Chris could get the words "You're nuts" out of his mouth, Willy was off and moving in the same direction as the two men.

"It's an adventure . . . it's an adventure . . .," Chris repeated to himself over and over.

Following the men involved doing three things at the same time: keeping the men in sight without being seen, making sure they didn't attract the attention of the guards, and hoping they didn't get lit up by the lights being used in the show. It occurred to Chris and Willy that the two men—whatever they were up to—had picked this time to do it, knowing that everyone else in the place would be preoccupied by the show. The soundtrack would provide good cover noise, and if their timing was good, the lights would focus attention away from where they were going. And it looked to the boys, as they crept along through the trees, as if they were going toward the back side of the great pyramid El Castillo.

Sure enough, the men emerged from the trees just on the far side of the pyramid. Right as they did that, the lights and narration focused on the Colonnade and the Ball Court, which meant that everyone else was now looking away from El Castillo. The men were indeed using the show as a distraction so they could move about undetected!

"Come on, Chris," Willy said, grabbing his friend's arm.

"They're going around the pyramid. We've got to see what they're up to."

Chris hesitated for a moment, then nodded. The two boys moved as quickly as possible.

Coming to the corner on the front side, they peered cautiously around the ancient stones. The men were nowhere to be seen. Sticking their heads out farther, they were almost blinded when the lights suddenly blazed on in front of El Castillo, bathing the entire structure in floodlights.

Wham! Willy slammed into Chris as the two of them threw themselves back into the shadows on the dark side. Both of them went down in a heap, just inches away from the brightly lit front wall. They lay there gasping, more from the shock than the collision.

They pushed themselves back up against the shadowed wall, holding very still. Neither one said a word, hoping that neither the men nor anybody else who had been looking their way had seen them. The taped narration went on, explaining how El Castillo had been built, the significance of the number of steps leading up it, and so on. No one had seen them.

After a few minutes—it seemed like an hour to the boys—the show once again shifted its attention away from the great pyramid, and they were in darkness. "Man, that was *close!*" whispered Willy. "Let's see if we can spot those two dudes again."

They crept forward again, peeking around the front wall once more. There they were! The two men had flattened themselves against the great front stairway, hidden from view as it protruded out in front of El Castillo. These two obviously had timed their work very tightly to take advantage of the show. They were now stealing quickly and quietly to the other side of the front stairway. Chris and Willy moved, too.

This time what they saw made them both stop, their mouths hanging open. There was a door leading into the pyramid—they had seen it earlier in the day, but it had not been open—with a large padlock hanging from it. The first man pulled a pair of special cutters from his shirt and cut the lock quickly and expertly. Pushing the door slightly open, he and his partner disappeared silently into the interior of El Castillo.

"Willy! There must be an inner chamber inside the pyramid or maybe a bunch of chambers. These guys are looking to steal stuff from in there," Chris quickly assessed. *"Now what do we do?"*

CHOICE ➡️

If Willy and Chris keep following them, turn to page 85.

If they go for help, turn to page 12.

The next day the group learned firsthand about another part of the world and what it's like to live there. Dave Metzler, the short-term project director for the northern Yucatán, showed them around and talked to them about the area, the people, and their history. He wanted the kids to understand that being there to perform a task was only a part of their visit. "Your work here will have a huge impact on these people. That's obvious," he said. "But we want them to have an impact on you, too. We don't want you to just come here to do your work and then return home and forget you ever came here. We want you to remember this part of the world—maybe for the rest of your life—not only the work you did."

After supper that evening everyone got together for a meeting to prepare for the start of the project the next day. Supper had been an adventure in itself. They had been served a favorite local dish called *pibil*—a corn tortilla stuffed with ground annatto seeds, shredded pork, and red onions and soaked in *pibil* sauce—along with rice and beans. Some of the kids had loved it, asking for several helpings. But Cheryl whispered to Jess, "If they serve us this stuff for two weeks, I'll lose all that weight I've been wanting to take off."

One of the other leaders, a college student named Matt, led everyone in singing. At first the songs were mostly for fun, and then they became more serious. After the singing and a time of introduction to more of their local coworkers, Jeff went over the few rules and the schedule one more time. There were groans as he reminded them that lights-out would be at ten o'clock and more groans as he announced that wake-up would be at six o'clock.

"You mean like . . . in the *morning?*" Sam asked as everyone laughed.

"Yes, I mean like in the morning," Jeff answered, smiling. "That's why it's important that everybody obeys the 'lights-out' rule. Believe me, we're going to be working very hard during the day, and you're going to need your sleep at night. And even if you don't think *you* do, everybody *else* needs it, so please cooperate. Anybody who gives me a hard time about the curfew will be soaked all night in *pibil* sauce and left out as a peace offering for these industrial-strength mosquitoes."

Jeff then reminded the group that they weren't on vacation but were there to accomplish a task. "Actually," he said, "I've found out that the task has turned out to be at least two tasks. But we're here to help, and that means being flexible. Our helpers here feel that our crew is too large to all work on the building we planned to put up. So some of you are going to be full-time on a children's project. I'm going to need volunteers." He paused, then grinned. "But before we do that, I want to get you excited about the special-event trips we'll be taking. Five days from now, and again on Sunday . . ."

As Jeff talked about some of the cool places they

were going to visit, Chris, Willy, Sam, Jessica, and Gonzo glanced at each other. Their traded looks said, Whatever we do, let's stick together!

CHOICE

If you can't wait to find out about the special trip on day five, turn to page 81.

To get started with the Ringers on the building project, turn to page 145.

Or, if the Ringers volunteer to help with the children's project, turn to page 53.

To go with the Ringers on the Sunday trip, turn to page 108.

Six o'clock came early to the travel-weary group of
Americans. Those who hadn't gotten right to bed paid an
extra price. But with some teasing from Jeff and the other
adults, all thirty or so of the work team made it to breakfast
on time.

Breakfast was another new experience: eggs and
potatoes with corn tortillas, and water or coffee to drink.
Recalling cereal commercials became a breakfast tradition
during the trip.

Another tradition that began the first morning Jeff
called "E-Time." Right after the meal, one of the adults read
some verses from the Bible and helped them all see how
God's Word applied to their lives. *E-Time* meant several
things: "Energizing Time," "Encouragement Time," and
"Eternity Time."

"Eternity Time?" asked Willy.

"Yeah," said Jeff, "what God says is true forever, and
we get to see how true it is today."

Beth, an adult from Jeff's church, led the first E-Time
by reading something from John 13 that Jesus said: "I have
given you an example to follow: do as I have done to you."
She explained that Jesus had just washed his disciples' feet.
She talked for a few minutes about how all Christians
should be servants like that. It was something they would
all hear and experience in many different ways in the days

ahead. After her brief talk, the group split up to spend a few minutes praying for the day's goals.

After E-Time the kids and adults grabbed their gloves, hats, bandannas, sunscreen, and tools, and headed for the work site. As they left the dorm, everyone was was silent as they experienced firsthand more sights and sounds of village life in the Yucatán Peninsula. . . .

There were the huts of the people, made out of bamboo and thatched roofs. There were few automobiles—and fewer paved streets. Some of the local people were already at work outside their homes— weaving, pounding corn, and doing many other things the group could only wonder about—as they sat near the smoking fire that had been used to cook their morning meal. Other villagers were heating water over other fires for various purposes. Chickens and roosters were everywhere, as were small, dark-skinned and darker-haired children. Some of the children just stared at the fair-haired and fair-skinned foreigners, and others ran to tell their families, yelling, *"Americanos! Americanos!"*

Finally they arrived at a hut next to a vacant lot. On the lot was a bare concrete slab and four large stacks of concrete blocks. Three Mexican men were walking across the slab with some tape measures and levels, and one held a spool of twine. As the Americans began spilling out of the vehicles, a short Mexican man came out of the hut, smiling warmly and spreading his arms in a welcoming gesture.

"Bienvenidos, hermanos y hermanas!" he called.

("Welcome, brothers and sisters!") He was Pastor Julio Celiz, Carlos's father and the pastor of the group of Christians meeting together as a church in San Felipe. Jeff and the other van drivers walked over to meet Julio and the other men, as did Matt and Robert Gentile, the contractor who had come to oversee the construction of the building. The men all extended handshakes and hugs, as was the local custom. It took Matt and Robert a minute to get the rhythm—handshake, hug, handshake—but by the time all the introductions had been given, they were old pros. Sam and Gonzo stood by to help with translating.

While the men were getting acquainted, the kids looked over the work site. In addition to the stacks of block, there was a large pile of sand, another of gravel, and several barrels filled with water. Off to the side there was already a small wooden structure. The team found out it was a tool and materials shed, where most of their equipment and supplies that needed to be kept inside would be stored.

Soon everyone gathered on the slab so they could receive some initial explanations and instructions.

Jeff spoke first. "Welcome to beautiful downtown San Felipe, your very own corner of paradise for the next two weeks." Jeff grinned. Tall by any standard, he looked positively treelike standing next to Julio and the other shorter Mexicans. Jeff introduced Pastor Julio as well as Juan, Pablo, and Jorge. These men were all members of the church and were taking precious time away from their normal work to help with the construction.

The Americans greeted their Mexican friends with handshakes and smiles. Some of the kids even tried their hand at saying, *"Hola, cómo está usted?"* ("Hello, how are you?") This brought smiles from the men and good-natured kidding from Sam and Gonzo.

Jeff continued. "This bare concrete slab we're standing on is going to be a church building in two weeks, Lord willing. These men and another group like ourselves poured this slab just a few weeks ago in preparation for our visit." The group then prayed, asking for God's help in the project and that he would use the building to minister to the people of San Felipe. Bob prayed in English, and Pastor Julio prayed in Spanish.

The group joined hands—Mexicans interspersed among the Americans, dark hands between white ones—and made a rough circle around the site. Without realizing it, they were a picture of God's kingdom on earth: different races, different colors, different languages, different ways of life—all united by belief in one God, one Lord and Savior, brothers and sisters in the Spirit.

When the prayer was over, Bob became the one in charge. "While most of us get busy moving blocks and mixing mortar, I need three volunteers for one important mission and three for another."

CHOICE ⇛

If the Ringers just stay with the main building team, turn to page 142.

Or, if some of the Ringers volunteer for mission one, turn to page 10.

To follow the Ringers who volunteer for mission two, turn to page 78.

Hold it!" said Jeff. "Look, Sam, I know you're trying to help this boy, and I know that's what we came here to do. But we can't help him this way. Besides, it doesn't look like this soldier is interested in your plan." He stopped, frustrated that they had come all this way only to have to give up on a child who obviously needed their help. "We'll have our pastor friend here look into this boy's situation to see if we can help in some other way while we're here."

Sam wasn't happy with this arrangement, but he didn't let that stop him from doing everything he could for Rodrigo while in Mexico.

The experience was a rude awakening for the kids from the U.S. They couldn't imagine that a child that young would be alone on the streets. But he wasn't the first needy child they would see. And many of them they would be able to help.

THE END

Some lessons come quickly, others take a while. Make other choices to discover some of the many lessons the Ringers learned and adventures they had along the way.

Willy did it. He shut his eyes, took a deep breath, and put his face in the wet, sticky concrete. *Plop!*

Everyone cheered, and when Willy pulled himself out of the mess, looking like a mud creature, they all broke up laughing at him. "Where's my twenty dollars?" he yelled.

"Oh, did I forget to say, 'Just kidding'?" said Matt. But when Willy started after him, Matt held out the money. "Get away, slime creature. Hey, somebody get a bucket and wash off the mud king!" Matt was concerned for himself as much as for Willy. Having worked construction, he knew that wet cement could actually cause burns if you touched it for a long time.

That little incident gave everyone a good laugh, gave Willy twenty dollars, and picked up the group's spirits. Matt told Jeff later it was the best twenty dollars he'd spent in a long time.

THE END

There are more adventures to be had! Turn to page 108 to catch up with the group on their day off.

The four of them took off after Sam's bag. Rounding another corner, they slammed into each other as they hesitated over which way to go.

Sam pushed his way to the front and yelled, "This way! Come on!" as he turned left down a walkway.

They hadn't even reached cruising speed when they heard a voice behind them yell, "Hey—gringos!" followed by laughter. Screeching to a halt and turning around, they saw a young Mexican guy standing in the walkway, holding Sam's bag and grinning. "Is this what you're looking for?"

Behind him was another, younger Mexican boy. As soon as the younger boy saw the four Ringers, he turned around and ran away, leaving the older one literally holding the bag.

Willy and Chris were ready to give chase again, but Sam yelled, "Gonzo, you dog! Give me my bag, or I'll pound you into a tortilla." Realizing they had been had, the four kids from Millersburg started laughing and walked over to meet Gonzalo Alvarez, Sam's friend from Miami.

"Gonzo, you jerk! How did you sneak up on us like that?" Sam was laughing and punching Gonzo's shoulder at the same time. "These are my friends Jessica, Willy, and Chris. Guys, this is Gonzo Alvarez, who *used* to be my friend."

"Nice to meet you," Gonzo said. "Sorry to make your

arrival here in Mérida so exciting, but I'm always looking for a chance to yank Samuel's chain. You should have seen your faces when you came around that corner!"

"Who was that little kid?" asked Willy.

"What kid?"

"There was a little kid behind you."

Gonzo shrugged. "Probably a *real* thief."

By this time Jeff Ellers and one of the young soldiers came quickly around the corner, looking concerned. "What happened? Is everything OK?"

"Yeah, everything's fine," Willy answered. "We just got introduced to Gonzo here in a way we won't soon forget."

Looking at the soldier, Gonzo said, *"Hay no problema, señor."* ("There is no problem, sir.") With a rather irritated look, the soldier turned and walked back to his post in front of the terminal.

"Let's go then, you guys. No more horsing around, OK? Young guys with loaded rifles make me nervous." Jeff led them back toward the waiting vans.

"We promise no more excitement—for now," said Sam. "Just remember, amigo," he said to Gonzo, "what goes around comes around. And don't *ever* call me gringo again," making his point with one more punch to Gonzo's shoulder.

In front of the terminal, several vans were waiting for the thirty kids and adults from the States. With their bags, cameras, purses, etc., it was quite a tight fit. As they drove through Mérida, they were all fascinated by the Spanish architecture, the quaint plazas, the huge cathedral, and the overall colonial feel of the town.

"This is like driving right through an old museum that hasn't been dusted in years!" commented Willy.

For most of the kids, it was their first trip out of the States, and everything was new and interesting. Cameras clicked and whirred.

After checking in with the mission headquarters, they headed northeast to San Felipe, about a hundred miles away. Once again the kids felt both excited and anxious heading into unfamiliar territory. Mérida was exotic, but Mérida was a fairly large city with many features of city life. San Felipe, on the other hand, was a small village of just a few hundred people and was located some distance away near the northern coast of the Yucatán. It would be another step into the unknown.

Finally the vans pulled up in front of a rather . . . *rustic*-looking building. The sign above the door read: *Bienvenidos a Príncipe de Paz Iglesia y Escuela* (Welcome to Prince of Peace Church and School). "Here we are, guys," Willy called out, "home, sweet home!"

"I hope it has running water," Jess mumbled.

"I have a feeling it'll have lots of running things," said Sam.

"OK," Jeff said. "Guys sleep in the rooms to the left, girls to the right."

Inside the school the team found a courtyard with shrubs and trees surrounded by a porch lined with doorways. The rooms were small, bare, concrete-block classrooms that had been converted to sleeping quarters. Bunk beds had been placed in each room, and all the school desks were pushed off to one side. There was one bathroom on each end with three toilets and two shower stalls. Electricity was a problem at times, so none of the kids had been allowed to bring hair dryers, curling irons, radios, or microwave ovens. To top it all off—no hot water!

"Somebody tell me again—why did I come on this trip?" Cheryl, Jess's roommate, mumbled under her breath. She was one of Jeff's youth group kids from Fairfax, and she and Jess had started talking on the flight and decided to room together.

"It wasn't for the luxury accommodations, that's for sure," Jess answered.

Over on the guys' side, a small problem had come up. Sam and Gonzo had grabbed the first available guys' room. Jeff had taken the last room, since he wanted to keep his equipment out of the traffic pattern. The other guys in his youth group had paired off and gotten their rooms, and Chris and Willy ended up in the room next to Jeff's.

There was one room left, and Danny Skotos, who had come with Jeff's group but wasn't really part of it, put his stuff in it. Danny preferred to keep to himself. Since radios weren't allowed on the trip, Danny, whose closest friend was his Walkman, had sat by himself on the plane and in the van, staring out the windows and saying very little. He was still wearing the denim jacket and dark glasses he'd worn on the plane, even though it was hot and dark inside.

Willy had a thought and got Chris's attention. "Hey, homey, something just hit me. Danny's in there by himself. Let's go see if he wants to pull his bunk in with us."

Chris and Willy had been best friends for years; the kids at Madison Junior High called them "Salt and Pepper."

They loved sitting up at night, shooting the breeze, talking about everything from girls to God. Chris had really been looking forward to getting to do that on this trip. . . .

CHOICE ⇒

If Willy and Chris decide to ask Danny to room with them, turn to page 51.

If they decide *not* to ask Danny to room with them, turn to page 107.

Jeff looked up, adjusted his glasses, and spoke. "I'm going to give him another chance. I realize it may set a bad precedent, but I think Danny's particular needs outweigh my other concerns. If I send him home, he's probably out of our influence forever. I *will* discipline him somehow—maybe make him stay here and do some clean-up type stuff while we take our next off-day—but I'm not going to send him home.

"I appreciate all of your input. . . . Matt, will you go get Danny?"

"Gladly," said Matt, with a smile.

While Matt was gone, Jeff and the others discussed how to discipline Danny. After a minute or so it was agreed that Jeff's first thought was a good one. On the next off-day, when the group was to go to Chichén Itzá, Danny would stay back and help with the cleaning, cooking, and laundry duties. By the time this was settled Matt was back with Danny.

"Please sit down, Danny," Jeff began in a very somber tone.

"Danny, what you did yesterday was very serious. You could have been hurt, lost, robbed, or even killed, and we might never have found you. You caused us all a lot of grief, and I don't appreciate that at all. If something *had* happened to you, who do you think your parents would have held responsible? *Me,* that's who.

"By all rights I ought to put you on the next plane

home to D.C. and let you explain to your folks why you're coming home without the rest of us. Before I tell you exactly what we *have* decided to do, do you have anything to say about what you've done?"

Danny looked around like a scolded puppy. After a few seconds of awkward silence, he spoke up very feebly.

"I'm sorry, Jeff . . . and I apologize to all the rest of you for causing you such trouble. I didn't mean to scare you. I wasn't trying to ruin your trip or your day off. I just wanted to get away from the way things are at home. . . . I wanted to get away from my *life*."

Jeff and the others couldn't help but feel compassion for a fifteen-year-old who hated his life that much. For the next ten minutes, Danny told them in soft, sorrowful tones about his home life—parents who used to fight all the time . . . his father's drinking . . . how his parents had called him stupid and lazy all the time and made fun of his friends . . . and then how his father had left them, and what it was like alone with his mom.

"Man, my whole life just hurts." With that final, bleak summation, Danny was again quiet.

"OK, Danny," Jeff resumed after a moment of silence. "OK. I'm sorry about how things are at home, and I'm glad you finally told us. You might be surprised to find out you're not the only one here with problems at home. At any rate, I do hope you understand that running away isn't going to solve your problems, and it creates a whole bunch of new ones for everyone else here.

"Now, if you will give me your word that you won't try anything like that again, I'll tell you what I've decided to do instead of sending you back. Is that a deal?"

Danny's face brightened for the first time in a long time. "I swear," he said, and he meant it.

"I won't send you home," Jeff proceeded. "Instead, you'll stay back here at Príncipe de Paz and help the locals with cleaning, laundry, and whatever else they need you to do while we all go to Chichén Itzá on our next off-day. Understood?"

"Yes sir," Danny replied.

"Danny, I hope you've learned something from this," Jeff continued. "And the main thing I hope you've learned is something the Bible calls *grace*. To put it simply, grace is when you get what you *don't* deserve, and when you *don't* get what you *do* deserve. You deserve to be sent home for breaking a rule that you clearly understood, and you understood the penalty for doing so. Before the trip is over, let's you and me talk about it again."

"OK," Danny said simply.

"OK, let's get moving. We're already late for work."

With that, the meeting broke up, and everyone went to get ready to head out to the work site, all wondering how things would work out with Danny.

THE END

To find out what happened to Danny, turn to page 16.

Or, for other adventures, turn back to page 26 or 1 and make different choices along the way.

Talking quickly among themselves, the seven of them debated the pros and cons of volunteering to help out. Even though they were all tired and were looking forward to an afternoon of fun, they couldn't shake the feeling that they ought to try to help this woman.

It was Jess who finally settled the issue for them. "Guys, what's the one thing they've been pounding into our heads this whole trip? *Servanthood.* How Jesus didn't come to be served but to serve. Is there any doubt in your minds what Jesus would do if he were standing here? I say we all go help this lady."

That pretty much settled it. The five boys and two girls could hardly disagree. Jessica spoke for them all: "Jeff, we'll go."

"Great," said Jeff. "And hey, I really appreciate you guys' attitude and your willingness to go the second mile. All right, everybody, we've got our work crew. Everybody else, finish cleaning up and let's get back to the dorm."

"Uh, Jeff, just a second." To everyone's surprise, it was Danny speaking. "Um, if it's OK, I'd like to go along and help out, too."

Jeff smiled, both surprised and gratified. "Sure, Danny. I think we can make room for you. That OK with you, Mr. Gentile?"

"Absolutely."

Bob, Chris, Willy, Jess, Cheryl, Sam, Gonzo, Carlos, and Danny—along with Pastor Julio—gathered wood and tools and took one of the vans over to the woman's house. The Americans had seen some pretty small, impoverished houses already on this trip, but this woman's home was far worse. It was the same kind of hut as most of the others in the village, but it wasn't made as well and hadn't been well kept up. It was all this woman, señora Hernandez, could do to work as a maid during the day and care for her children in the evenings.

Pastor Julio greeted her and explained what they were there to do. Overwhelmed, tears welled up in her eyes, and she kept repeating to them, *"Gracias! Dios les bendiga!"* ("Thank you! God bless you!")

Bob put the team to work right away. They only had one afternoon, and they needed to hurry. He decided they would simply tear down the old hut—after the family had pulled their few belongings out—and build a better wooden one in the same spot.

He gave out instructions quickly and precisely. "Willy, you and Chris cut 12 two-by-fours of exactly eight feet. Cheryl, you and Jess haul that stuff off to the side—she can decide how to dispose of it later. Danny, how about you and Carlos unloading all the other wood from the van? Sam, you and Gonzo go with Pastor Julio and help him get the stuff on this list from the storage shed back at the site, OK?"

It was hard, but the group worked together like a real team. By 6:30 that evening, señora Hernandez and her three little ones had a new, roomier, sturdier home. They were absolutely ecstatic about what the group had done for them.

"OK, guys, good job," Bob said to them as they admired their handiwork. "You can be real proud of what you accomplished today. I don't think this lady will ever forget what you've done for her and her children."

"You, too, Mr. Gentile," said Chris. "You're all right for an old man."

They drove back to the dorm, exhausted but feeling very good about what they had done.

THE END

Turn to page 16.

Listen, guys," said Jessica as they pulled tools from the trailer, "I've never done anything important like this by myself! I mean, I helped my dad build stuff, but I'm not real good with tools, and I'm just sure I'm gonna make a big mistake and have the roof come crashing down on our heads."

Gonzo looked at her for a moment, trying to decide what to say. "Look at me, Jess. Do I seem like Joe Carpenter to you? And you know something else, when Sam and I were younger, he once tried to tell me that a hammer was used to hit the nails on the ends of your fingers. He told me *hammer* was an Indian word for 'hard thing that crush thumb'!"

"No, that's not what I said," Sam countered. "What I said was *hammer* meant 'hard thing that give Gonzo bump on head'!"

Jess threw up her hands in surrender. "That does it—everyone who comes to this church will have to wear a hard hat!"

Actually, once Bob helped them measure and put the first truss together, they were gaining in confidence. Like the repetition in building the block walls of the building, once a single truss was made, it had to be copied over and over, exactly. Each truss formed a wide, low triangle, with long outside pieces and many short braces.

By the end of the first day, there were three trusses done. Each day after that, the pile grew larger until the block walls were up. It was quite a thrill for Jess, Sam, and Gonzo to see their trusses lifted onto the building walls. In less than two hours, the trusses it had taken days to build were all nailed in place and ready for the wavy metal sheeting that would form the roof.

"Still worried about the roof caving in?" whispered Sam to Jess the first time they walked in the door. The others were already attaching the roof sheets.

"No," she said looking up at the intricate pattern of their work, "I thinks it's beautiful. . . . And we built them!"

THE END

A real sense of accomplishment comes from learning a new skill and then using it to help others. Jess's parents could hardly believe it when she told them what she had done, but they agreed that her pictures showed some great-looking trusses!

Sam, Gonzo, Willy, and Cheryl really enjoyed carrying out their task. While Sam did not know the village or the people like Carlos did, he had no trouble finding out which homes they should visit. There were children everywhere. The people of San Felipe were very friendly and helpful to these four visitors, so much so that Cheryl commented on the difference between this culture and the one she was used to.

"Can you imagine going through a strange neighborhood like this back home? I'd be scared to death to do this!"

"Yeah," agreed Willy, "and I don't think the people would be quite so friendly."

"Majorly insane understatement, Kimosabe," added Sam.

Beth was right—Cheryl and Willy attracted lots of attention just by being there, perhaps because Willy was black. They made an interesting team: one black, one white, and two Hispanics, walking through the dirt streets and adobe huts of San Felipe. The morning flew by as they went from house to house visiting. By the time lunchtime rolled around they had worked up an appetite and were satisfied with their efforts.

The children's Bible school was a tremendous success. Every day at least fifty children would show up by one-thirty, eager to get started on another lesson and series of activities. Beth and the volunteers taught the children some of the main truths of the Bible in lots of creative ways: reading stories, singing songs, playing games, giving puppet shows, and doing simple crafts. Many of the children wanted to invite Jesus to be their Lord and Savior, too. So, with the help of one of the bilingual people, Beth and her helpers explained to them how to do that. The new believers were given Spanish New Testaments with their names written in them and notes from the American kids who had become friends with them.

Many of the kids made deep and lasting friendships with their new Mexican *amigos.* Several of the Ringers continued to write them letters long after the trip was over.

THE END

If you're not sure what the Mayan mystery is, turn to page 1 and make different choices along the way.

Or, to read about the end of the trip, turn to page 16.

Even though Danny seemed like a loner and was hard to get to know, the whole point of this trip was serving God by serving others. They had come to serve God by helping the Mexican believers in the village of San Felipe, but maybe God wanted them to start serving right there with another teammate. It might not be easy, but both of them had heard Pastor Whitehead (back in Millersburg) say that growing in Christ often called for that.

"You know, sometimes even *you* have good ideas," Chris said, smiling. "Let's go ask him."

They walked over to Danny's room, acted as if they were knocking on the door, although it was wide open, and stepped in. Danny was just putting his duffel bag on the extra bunk.

Chris leaned against the door, his arms folded, as he pretended to scope out the room. "Hey, nobody gets a private room around here," Chris said with mock seriousness.

"Yeah," Willy chimed in, picking up on Chris's acting and trying to look tough, "nobody but Jeff, and he's the main dude." Then he smiled. "But seriously, you want to come stay in our room? We'll help you pull your bed down there."

Danny just looked at the two of them for a moment.

52

He wasn't sure what to say—it wasn't often that people tried to be nice to him.

If Danny decides to room with Willy and Chris, turn to page 150.

If Danny turns down their offer, turn to page 94.

After they found out that the children's project involved helping with VBS, the Ringers decided to volunteer. They figured they had something to teach, with all their talks with Mr. Whitehead. "Besides," reasoned Sam, "it means less sweating."

"Samuel! Gonzalo! Willy! Chris!" Carlos's voice called out as he came walking quickly up the dirt road of San Felipe to the work site. The Mexican boy had met the Ringers the night before, and they had already become acquainted. Now it was about ten o'clock, and the morning was quite warm. The work team had already begun the first stages of the "grunt work" involved in mixing concrete and laying block for the church they were building, but those who had volunteered for the children's project were standing around awkwardly. Carlos's arrival was good news to them.

The five boys, along with Jessica and Cheryl, were just greeting each other and making small talk when Jeff came walking over to them with Beth, another adult from Jeff's church. *"Buenos días,* Carlos," Jeff said, smiling at his own weak attempt to speak Spanish. *"Cómo estás?"*

"Good morning, don Jeff," Carlos replied with a grin of his own. "Welcome to my village." Even though it was poor and unremarkable, San Felipe was home, and Carlos was proud of it. The fact that thirty American Christians believed San Felipe was important enough to spend two weeks there, working and helping the church, added to Carlos's sense of pride.

"Beth and I want to explain how you can help us with the children's project this morning," Jeff said. "We need a few of you—including Carlos, Gonzo, and Sam, who have been volunteered—to go out into the village and go to the people's homes to tell them about the Bible school we're running for the children."

One of Beth's specific duties on the trip was to head up the children's project, which included a two-week Bible school. She had brought along puppets, games, prizes, films, and lots of other items to make listening to Bible stories interesting to the children of San Felipe.

"What are Chris, Jessica, Cheryl, and I going for, Jeff?" asked Willy. "It's not like we can help with translating or anything."

Beth responded, "Willy, you saw how much attention our group attracted just by driving out here yesterday. These little kids have never seen anything quite like this group before. They are fascinated with us and are very curious about why we're here. I know you four can't speak the language, but just having you go along makes a real positive statement about our interest in the children—and you draw a lot of attention. You're sort of like walking billboards for the Bible school. We'll put two of you with Carlos and the other two with Sam or Gonzo. They can do all the talking. What do you say?"

Jessica, Cheryl, Willy, and Chris stood for a minute, talking this over. Jessica and Cheryl were both shy by nature and a little reluctant to go walking up to people's homes, especially in Mexico. On the other hand, they did like the idea of helping the Bible school and spending time with the local children. They decided that as long as Sam, Gonzo, and Carlos were doing the talking, they would go along.

But Willy and Chris were suddenly having second thoughts. Like all the boys on the trip, they had envisioned long hours of hard labor in the hot sun, helping to *build a building*. They had also imagined going home and telling their friends about their heroic construction efforts. The thought of inviting children to Bible school was not quite as macho.

But there *was* a bit of adventure in going out into this strange village and getting to see firsthand how these people lived. . . .

CHOICE

If Chris and Willy decide to stay and help with the construction work after all, turn to page 74.

If they decide to go into the village, turn to page 120.

Jeff sighed. "I'm going to send him home," he said solemnly. "I don't feel like I've got any choice. I told everyone that leaving the group and wandering off without permission was a major no-no and that it would get you sent home. If I don't follow through, the rest of the group will think the rules don't mean anything. I can't have that in a setting like this. I'm responsible for these kids.

"I'm going to put him on the next plane home."

Matt spoke up. "Jeff, I understand what you're saying, and I respect your decision. But I want to say that I really disagree with it. This is an extremely hurting kid, and I think we need to cut him some slack here."

"OK, Matt," Jeff replied. "I appreciate your honesty. Let's agree to disagree on this, OK? But I need you to back me when we tell the rest of the group. *And* Danny."

The next several minutes were spent in planning how to carry out Jeff's decision. Beth agreed to call the airlines; Bob offered to drive to the airport. Matt volunteered to get Danny and bring him back to the meeting room so Jeff and the others could tell him what they had decided. Mrs. Jordan offered to call Danny's parents and break the news to them, but Jeff reluctantly declined. "That's my responsibility," he said, dreading it.

Before they scattered to carry out their duties, Jeff

asked the group to pray. To Willy's surprise, Jeff asked him to pray for Danny, too.

"OK," Willy said. "Lord, I know Danny must be really upset. I pray that you would show him his . . . uh, sin . . . and help him turn to you instead. Lord, please help him with whatever it is he's running away from. Show him that he needs to quit living like this, shutting people out, and that he needs to give his life to Jesus. I pray in Jesus' name. Amen."

"Thanks, Willy," said Jeff. "OK, Matt—would you go get Danny? If the rest of you would stay put so he knows it's a group decision, I'd appreciate it. Willy, you and Chris—you guys want to stay?"

"I'll stay," Chris said after a moment's thought.

"Me too," added Willy.

Danny had been sitting on his bunk, his things packed, prepared for the bad news. Matt tried not to give it away with his face, but he knew he probably did anyway. They walked into the meeting room together and sat down.

"Danny," Jeff began, "what you did yesterday was very dangerous. It was foolish, risky, and very self-centered. You have no idea how much anxiety you caused all of us, including me. If something had happened to you, *I* would have been held responsible. I simply can't have someone on the project who could put the whole team in jeopardy like that.

"I'm sorry, Danny, but I've got to send you home. If we can change your plane ticket without costing any more money, we will. If not, you or your mom will be responsible for whatever else we have to pay. I know that sounds harsh, but you knew those were the rules when you signed on to go on this project. Do you have anything you want to say at this point?"

Danny sat still for a few seconds, staring down at his hands. Then he shook his head and said, "No, I guess not. I'm sorry I made you all worry—that wasn't what I was trying to do. I just . . . it's just that, things are so bad at home, I just thought this was my chance to maybe get away. . . . I'm sorry."

"Danny," Jeff said in a softer tone, "we're not doing this because we think you're a terrible person. Everyone in this room cares about you and wants the best for you. That's why we've made this decision. As you go back, please think about two things: One, that your actions have consequences. This is a direct result of your actions yesterday. And two: We love you, Danny. No one here hates you. When we get back to the States, *please* come and talk about stuff at home—whenever you are ready. I really want to help."

Danny simply nodded.

The flight left just before noon, which gave Danny several hours to think about what he had done. Jeff and the others hoped and prayed it would help him see that they really did care.

THE END

For a different ending to Danny's story, turn to page 41.

The soldier kept shaking his head no to whatever Sam was saying. The dark-skinned American was pleading, but it did little good.

Rodrigo, the little thief, hung his head as the soldier led him away. "I'm sorry, señores," said the young man in uniform, "but he must go to jail."

"To *jail?*" asked Jessica, hardly believing what she had just heard.

"That little kid?" added Willy.

The soldier looked back at the group behind him. He was not enjoying his job. "This one no have mother and father, señores. Live in streets, get in trouble many time."

It looked like the boy realized they were speaking about him, for he hung his head in sadness, and he didn't resist when the soldier led him away.

Sam bent over and grabbed his duffel angrily. He looked off in the distance as his eyes misted over. Suddenly, he dropped his bag and ran after the soldier.

Willy picked up his bag. "That Sam! If his stuff makes it through the trip, it'll be a miracle. Guess we'd better find out what he's up to now." Willy followed Sam as the others trailed behind.

Back in front of the terminal they found Sam talking with the young soldier, who was already seated in a Jeep with the boy and another soldier. As they came near, Sam reached out, ruffled the boy's hair, and said something to him as the Jeep pulled away from the curb. When the boy turned to look at Sam, the others could see from the two streaks down the boy's cheeks that he had been crying, but now there was a tiny smile under his still-sad eyes as the Jeep disappeared from sight.

"Well, Sam, you must have said something nice to the boy to make him smile like that on his way to jail," said Jeff. "You'd better tell me so I'll know what to say if I have to send some of you to jail during this trip!"

"I think I told Rodrigo something he never expected me to say," said Sam.

"What's that?" asked the others.

"I told Rodrigo I wouldn't forget him in jail and that I would do what I could to help him," said Sam.

Jeff's forehead furrowed a little. He could tell that Sam cared about the boy, but he wasn't sure what they could do. Finally he sighed and said, "That was a very kind thing to say, Sam, but I don't know if we have the time, or even a way, to help this boy."

"Well, I tried not to promise more than I could do. But isn't this trip about helping people? Isn't Rodrigo a kid who needs help?" Sam's voice was rising as he expressed his concern.

Jeff took a deep breath before speaking. "You're right, this is a trip about helping people. And God may give us even more opportunities than we planned. But let me tell you, our plans will keep us busy enough. Right now we need to get to the mission headquarters and touch base with our contact, then head for San Felipe and the work

we already committed to. Once we're there, we can pray
for Rodrigo. And maybe we'll look into what else we can
do for him."

Sam looked disappointed and agitated but said
nothing.

Some of the others thought Sam was being a little
bullheaded. Jeff was right—their real purpose was to do
the work they'd already said they'd do.

If Sam listens to Jeff, turn to page 100.

If Sam insists, turn to page 125.

DAAANNNNY!" Willy shouted at the top of his lungs as
he tried to turn around. The wet clay under his feet was
slick as ice, and he went down hard. Next thing he knew,
he was almost under the muddy water. He pushed himself
up, spitting out a mouthful. He was taking a breath to shout
again when, to his horror, he saw the hut collapse in slow
motion.

The roof groaned loudly as the walls became mud and
could no longer support the weight. Pieces of the roof fell
apart and began floating away, and in seconds, all that was
left of the hut was one corner of the walls with a broken
door hanging from a single hinge. The door was swinging
as water rushed under it.

Then Willy felt Chris's hands under his arms, helping
him to his feet. They rushed toward the mud pile that had
been their shelter a few moments before. For some strange
reason, Willy swung open the door as if to enter the hut
that was no longer there. He hardly had time to wonder
what he would—or wouldn't—find inside.

There, sitting in the mud, with his back against the
only part of the wall still upright, was Danny. He was
shaking uncontrollably. Slowly he looked up at the two
dripping boys standing in the doorway. His eyes were filled
with fear. He put his hands over his face and began to
weep.

Without speaking, Willy and Chris each took one of Danny's arms and pulled him to his feet. "We gotta get outa here," said Willy firmly. "The rest of this place could come down any second."

Still holding Danny, they led him away from the hut toward the village. Just as quickly as it had come, the storm ended.

The three hadn't gone far when Danny slowed down and said, "Thanks. I'm OK."

As soon as the rain had stopped, Willy and Chris had realized how cold they were. "It looks to me like we're all shaking like leaves," said Willy, trying to lighten the mood.

"Yeah, but you guys are just cold. I was scared to death!" said Danny. "What would have happened if I had been alone?"

"Don't even think about it!" said Chris. "Besides, if there's one thing I think you should learn on this trip, it's that you can't ever be alone as long as Jesus is around."

"I'm not sure I understand what you're saying, Chris, but I will say that Jesus is becoming more than just a name to me."

"Well, keep your eyes, ears, and heart open, Danny. Jesus will find a way to get through to you!" Willy said. "Now let's hustle back to the work site. There's probably a real mess to help clean up! Besides, it's almost lunchtime!" he added, taking off at a slow jog, just to keep warm.

Chris and Danny smiled at each other, enjoying the friendship between them that was beginning to grow. Then they ran after Willy.

64

THE END

Danny and the others had many experiences on this trip. If you haven't read the others, be sure to turn back and make different choices along the way.

Jeff!" Chris yelled as he and Willy hurried over to where Jeff was standing. "Willy and I need to . . . uh, run to the bathroom, OK?"

"OK," said Jeff. "I guess when señor Montezuma calls, you better answer."

"Thanks!" Chris and Willy took off running toward the front entrance.

"Poor guys," Beth said, watching them run off.

"If I'm right," Chris said as he and Willy skidded to a halt near the front gate, "this will explain where our buddy Carlos went after we got inside tonight."

"You got it, dude," panted Willy. "It sure is interesting how he came in with the rest of us and then disappeared before the show started."

The two wanna-be detectives looked around the entrance area, trying to figure out where Carlos might reemerge. They wanted to be able to see him before he saw them in case he might still be wearing the costume they thought they had seen him wear on top of the temple. But as they were positioning themselves to get the first glimpse of their suspect, Carlos came walking up behind them. Willy and Chris were both so intent on playing Sherlock Holmes that neither one of them heard him approach.

"Hola, gringos!" Carlos said, leaning in close behind them. *"Qué pasa?"*

Willy and Chris both jumped.

"Hey!" yelped Willy. "Where in the world did you come from?"

"And what are you doing sneaking up on us like that?" asked Chris, recovering from the surprise. "Where have you been, Carlos?"

"Sorry, señores," Carlos said with mock innocence. "I no speak English."

Before they could say any more, Jeff and the rest of the crew strolled up.

"Señor Ellers, I think you better have a little talk with Chris and Willy," Carlos called out. "They were looking very suspicious just now." His accent was still thick, but Carlos had gotten better at speaking English after spending the week with the team. "I think you need to question them about what they were doing."

"Is that right?" Jeff asked with the same sly grin as Carlos. "You know, these two have been nothing but trouble ever since this trip began."

"All right, what gives?" asked Chris. Whatever Carlos had been up to, it was obvious Jeff had been in on it. "Tell us the truth, Jeff. Where was Carlos tonight during the show?"

Jeff chuckled and then said, "Well, Carlos, I think it's time you let them in on your secret."

"OK," replied Carlos. "If you want me to, I will."

Jeff told everyone to sit down there on the tiled floor of the entrance area. Carlos spoke to the group in English, and with a good bit of assistance from Sam and Gonzo, this is what he told them:

"You all heard tonight the story of my people, the Maya, and where we came from and how we settled this area. Much of what you heard is true, and some of it is legend.

"You also heard the story of Kukulcán, the great ruler and statesman who led the first settlers here to Chichén Itzá. There is a great deal of truth in his story, although some of what the narrator said tonight must be taken as myth.

"Most of you know that I was orphaned as a baby and that Pastor Julio and his wife took me in and raised me as their son. They were always truthful with me, and I knew that they were not my birth parents. I do not know much about my parents, except that they were descendants of the Maya.

"The old woman who brought me as a baby to Pastor Julio's house told him that I was a descendant of Kukulcán himself."

The group was totally silent as they listened to Carlos, captivated by his story. When he got to this point, however, there was an audible gasp from the group.

"I do not know if it is true," Carlos continued. "The woman died long before I was old enough to ask her about my parents. But most of the people of San Felipe seem to think it is true, and they give me respect far beyond what someone my age normally receives."

"So was it you up on top of the temple tonight, Carlos?" Willy asked, sounding like an interrogator.

"That must remain my mystery," Carlos said slyly.

The place erupted with the protests of the kids demanding to know. Jeff looked at Carlos and said, "I think you're going to have to tell them, Carlos."

"OK, OK," Carlos said with a laugh. "I will tell you." He paused, for dramatic effect. Carlos may not have had a great command of the English language, but he, like many Mexican men, had a flair for telling a story.

"Yes, it was me."

"I knew it!" yelled Chris. He and Willy slapped each other a high five.

"How did you do that stunt at the end, Carlos?" Beth asked. "It looked like you dove right off the edge of the building and then disappeared."

"I *really* can't tell you that, Beth," Carlos said, looking uneasy. "The guys that run the show won't let me tell anything about that. They probably wouldn't even like my telling you what I did already, but they don't speak any English, so I guess they won't know."

"How often do you do that stunt, Carlos?" Cheryl asked.

"Not very often," Carlos replied. "A couple of guys here get paid to do it. Whenever I do it for them, it gives them a night off."

They talked for a little while longer that night. Then Jeff and the other adults herded everyone back into the vans, and several of the kids fought over who got to sit by Carlos. Not surprisingly, Jessica won.

"Cool," she said as they pulled out onto the Mexican highway. "A real live connection to history!"

THE END

Turn to page 16.

Chris and Willy were surprised at Danny's rejection—and, to be honest, a little hurt—but there was really nothing they could do if Danny's mind was made up. "Well, we tried," said Chris. "I guess that's what's important."

Willy just shrugged. He was a little hurt, but he still felt sorry for Danny. He just didn't understand why Danny kept to himself so much.

Oh well. Maybe he'd find out later. . . .

Turn to page 26.

Jess decided to respect Sam and Gonzo's secret. That's what she would want them to do for her.

A moment later the three were pulling tools out of the trailer when Gonzo spoke. "Jess, have you done anything like this before?" He pulled out a saw and handed it to Sam to carry.

"You mean build trusses?" asked Jessica.

"Yeah," added Sam, watching how she handled the tools.

"Well, I've never built trusses, but I can tell you we won't need that saw you just pulled out. It's a hacksaw, and it's mostly used for cutting pipe."

"I knew that," Gonzo muttered under his breath as he took the saw back from Sam and replaced it in the trailer.

Jess noticed he was embarrassed and figured that that must have been what the boys were whispering about. "Look," Jess pointed out, "my dad built our house himself, and since I don't have any big brothers, I got to help him. I learned a lot! It was kind of like this situation. I'm sure we're all going to learn new things this trip. Like, I sure wish I could speak Spanish like you guys."

"You keep teaching me about saws and stuff, and I'll teach you some Spanish," offered Gonzo.

"I guess it can't be too hard," said Jess. "I mean, look at all those little kids around here. They're all speaking

Spanish!" They chuckled over that one as they gathered their tools and got ready for their first lesson in the art of truss making.

THE END

Everyone on the trip learned from everyone else. That's one of the ways God works. He has made us so we need each other. Make sure you go back and try all the choices so you don't miss out on any part of this Ringer adventure!

Willy and Chris slipped out of their chairs and walked back up the darkened pathway toward the entrance. It never crossed their minds to tell anyone where they were going, since they were only intending to walk back to the bathrooms to see where Carlos might have gone. They felt sure he had to be somewhere between where they had been sitting and the entrance because the rest of the area was off-limits after dark.

They walked into the men's room. No sign of Carlos. They stepped back out, took a quick look around the entrance area, and decided he wasn't anywhere around there. Shaking his head, Chris said to Willy, "Might as well go back to our seats—he isn't around here. Maybe we just missed him and he's sitting out there with everybody else."

Willy nodded his agreement.

They were almost at the end of the path when something caught Willy's eye off to the right. He stopped, grabbed Chris by the shoulder, and motioned for him to stop and look. The two men who had been sitting at the back of the section were just disappearing behind some trees and moving in the general direction of the great pyramid El Castillo.

"Willy!" Chris rasped. "What do you think they're doing?"

"I don't know," Willy whispered. "Should we . . ."

"Follow them?" Chris finished Willy's thought.

Willy's eyes burned with a look Chris had seen before, and Chris knew what Willy was thinking: *adventure!*

They had to make their decision in a matter of seconds or they would never be able to find the two men disappearing into the dark Yucatán night.

CHOICE

If Chris and Willy follow the men, turn to page 23.

If they decide against it, turn to page 92.

Chris and Willy looked at each other, both wanting the other to make a decision. They wanted the company of the others, but they also thought about how it might sound back at home. The uncertain future seemed stronger than the present, so they shrugged their shoulders.

"I think we'll skip this part," said Chris.

"Yeah, maybe we can help some later, once the building is going up," added Willy.

But as soon as they turned away from their friends, they both knew they were making a poor choice. Before either of them could say something, however, they noticed someone familiar moving away from the building site. Danny was, as usual, just about to slip off by himself when Chris and Willy caught up with him.

"Yo, Danny," Chris called. "Wait up, will you?"

Looking distinctly uncomfortable, Danny stopped by one of the small adobe huts. He didn't say anything, but his look showed that he was uneasy. Willy remembered something about the night before. "Hey, didn't you volunteer to help with the children's project last night?"

Danny scowled at them and said, "Yeah . . . , I guess I did. You guys did, too. So how come you're not off with the others?" He nodded toward Beth and her helpers who were beginning to walk away.

It was Willy and Chris's turn to look uncomfortable.

Danny continued, "Look, I volunteered 'cause I thought I could get away on my own and check out these people. They're so different from us. I wonder what it'd be like to live here."

"Now that you mention it," said Willy, "that sounds like a neat part of doing this kid's thing—seeing how people really live here. But I know Jeff won't want you wandering off alone. Let's go together!"

At first, Danny just went along with the idea. But a few minutes later, as they wandered through the dusty pathways in the village, surrounded by children of all sizes, Danny realized he wouldn't have been alone anyway. Plus, since none of them could speak Spanish, it was kind of nice to "not understand anything" together. They decided the best they could do for the children's project was to point back toward the building site and say *"Mañana"* ("tomorrow"). They were hoping the kids would realize they were being invited to show up the next day.

The boys got to enjoying themselves so much they didn't notice how far they were from the building site. If fact, they came to the edge of the village, where the huts were farther apart. They also hadn't been watching the skies, which suddenly became dark. All of a sudden, the kids who had been following them disappeared. They seemed to know what was coming.

"Should we head back?" Chris asked.

Willy and Danny both looked upset that their fun might be interrupted.

"So it rains some. What difference can that make?" said Danny.

Chris tried again. "Listen, it's almost lunchtime. If we hurry back, we might miss the rain but still get fed instead of wet!"

The boys huddled to decide.

"Come on, guys," said Danny, "we've been telling the kids about the children's thing as well as we could. Let's do a little more exploring before we go back."

Willy was about to say something when a huge raindrop landed on his nose. Within seconds, the skies opened up with thunder, lightning, and a sudden deluge. The boys looked for the closest shelter they could find. Nearby was an old empty hut with the broken door hanging by one hinge.

"Maybe we can get out of the rain in there," shouted Chris over the storm. There were no arguments. A few seconds later, already soaked to the skin, the boys were crowded against the mud wall in the hut. The roof leaked badly, but the boys were able to avoid the worst of the drips.

"This can't last too long," said Danny hopefully, pushing his wet hair to one side. There was almost no light in the hut. The wind was blowing hard, shaking the thatch roof like a baby rattle. Minutes later, with the storm still howling, the boys all thought they heard some shouting outside.

"Could that be the rest of the team looking for us?" Chris wondered out loud.

"Naw," answered Danny. "Even if they realized we were gone right away, it would still take them longer to come looking for—"

Willy interrupted him and shouted, "Did you feel that? This thing is moving!"

The far corner of the hut buckled like a sand castle being hit by a wave. Through the large hole the boys could see water rushing by. The hut groaned and began to tilt toward the hole.

Chris and Willy leaped for the door. Ankle-deep water was flowing swiftly around both sides of the hut. They turned toward the village to make their escape when Willy realized Danny was not with them.

CHOICE

If Willy goes back for Danny, turn to page 131.

If he just shouts for him, turn to page 62.

Since Willy, Chris, and Danny had already volunteered, Gonzo and Sam decided to work together on the other job. Carlos seemed like the obvious choice to make up the third part of their team, but Carlos told them he would only be able to help for a little while that day. So the dynamic duo needed another partner.

Both of them turned toward Jessica at the same time.

"How about you, Jess? Want to help us on our mission?" asked Sam.

"What is it?" asked Jess, flattered they would even notice her.

"Don't you know we're not allowed to ask what we're volunteering for before we do it around here?" said Gonzo.

"OK, OK," said Jessica with a laugh. "If I have to keep busy, it might as well be with you guys."

"I'll take that as a show of confidence," Sam said colorfully.

Bob rubbed his hands together to wind up for his instructions. "You three get to learn the art of making trusses."

The three kids looked at each other.

"Trusses are a form of public transportation, right?" Sam joked.

Bob laughed. "No. Trusses are the wooden frames that hold up a roof. I'll show you how to make them. You'll need to make twenty-four of them by the time we get the walls built."

"Right, chief," said Gonzo. "Where do we start?"

"Get out the tape measures you each brought, then take from the tool trailer some saws, hammers, nails, and the sawhorses we brought along. Set them in that open area and I'll be right with you."

The builder turned his attention to getting the concrete-block crew going, then caught up with the truss gang. In the meantime, there seemed to be some discussion going on. . . .

CHOICE ⇒

If Jess is having second thoughts about building trusses, turn to page 47.

If Sam and Gonzo are talking about Jess, turn to page 5.

Chris and Willy wandered back to their room. They were tired and restless at the same time. They finished unpacking. Getting ready for bed took much longer than necessary, since brushing their teeth turned into an "ugly face" contest. Then their game of "nuclear pillow missiles in the dark" got a little loud.

But they finally heard Jeff's voice next door say, "Gentlemen, I will derive great joy from waking you up first tomorrow morning. And I still have the rest of tonight to dream up a way to do it that will make it a truly memorable experience!"

They heard him chuckle at the end, and they weren't sure if he was trying to be funny or laughing because he had already decided what he was going to do to them. They decided to quiet down and get to sleep.

CHOICE

Turn to page 29.

The first three days of work followed the same pattern: up at six, breakfast, devotions (or "E-Time," as they called it), and then off to the site. Mornings and late afternoons were spent working on the building, and in the early afternoons Beth (an adult from Jeff's church) and another four or five of the kids would hold Bible school for the local kids.

The project was on schedule, but it was difficult work. None of the team had ever worked so hard. Cheryl swore that when she got home, she would hug her air conditioner, her water heater, and McDonald's.

The hard work had a pleasant side effect, though: it drew the group together. Although not everyone knew each other when the trip began, they were starting to act and feel like a team—a family.

All except Danny.

Danny kept to himself, rubbing shoulders with the others only when necessary. Even Willy and Chris weren't having much success in drawing him out, even though they tried. It was obvious that Danny had not come on this trip because he wanted to.

Day five was a day off! After all their hard work, everyone was especially looking forward to the sightseeing: a visit to the Mayan ruins at Tulum, situated on the east coast of the

Yucatán Peninsula. There would also be some small markets where the kids could spend some of their newly exchanged pesos. Everyone was excited, to say the least.

They arrived at Tulum at noon. They explored the ancient coastal city where the Maya had once lived and worked. Though not a large ruin site, Tulum was very popular with tourists because it was right on the coast. The beautiful blue waters of the Caribbean and a white, sandy beach were visible from the ancient city.

After an hour and a half at the Tulum ruins, everyone piled back into the vans to drive back up the coast to a beautiful lagoon called Xel Ha ("Shell Ha"). Here the group swam and snorkeled in the clear waters. Xel Ha was fed by fresh water springs, but it also opened into the Caribbean, giving it a mix of fresh and salt water. With its unusual rock formations and plentiful tropical fish, it was like nothing any of the group had ever seen before.

"This place looks like something you'd see at Disney World," observed Willy.

"Imagine that. God could make a place as beautifully as Walt Disney," Matt said, teasing.

All too soon it was time to leave Xel Ha and make the trip back to the dorm at Príncipe de Paz. Jeff went to each van to get a head count.

He came up one short. "Who's missing?" Jeff called out. "Everybody check and see if the person who sat next to you on the way over is there now."

It hit Chris and Willy at the same time: *Danny!* They hadn't seen him since they left Tulum.

"Jeff!" Chris yelled. "Where's Danny?"

A quick check through the other vans confirmed that Danny was missing. No one could remember seeing him since they had gone to Tulum.

"What do we do now, guys?" Jeff asked the other adults. "He could have just gotten left behind at Tulum, or . . ." He paused.

"Or he could have run off," Beth said, finishing the thought for him.

Jeff nodded. Obviously, someone had to go back to Tulum and look—and soon, before they ran out of daylight.

"OK," Jeff started, trying to sound more confident than he felt. "I'll take one of the vans and go back to Tulum to look for Danny. Everybody else head back to San Felipe—and pray we find Danny quickly."

"Do you want to take Carlos with you, Jeff?" asked Matt.

"Good idea. Yeah, I'll need Carlos with me for sure—and Sam, too. That way if we have to split up to look for him, I'll have two translators. Matt, I guess you'd better come, too, and let's take Chris and Willy, too, since they probably know him better than anybody else at this point."

"What about me, Jeff?" asked Gonzalo.

"Gonzo, you go back with the big group. They'll need a translator along with them, too. Beth, you go back with them, too, OK? Mrs. Jordan, why don't you come with me, just in case. Jess and Cheryl—you want to come with us or go back with the rest?"

Jess and Cheryl said they wanted to help look for Danny, too.

"All right," Jeff continued. "Bob, you take charge of

getting everybody squared away when you get back. Go ahead and do lights-out at ten, just like normal. Hopefully, we won't be too far behind you. Everybody clear on what we need to do?" Jeff didn't feel too clear himself.

"Jeff," Beth spoke up. "Let's get everyone together to pray for Danny before we go, OK?"

Jeff readily agreed. Everyone spilled out of the vans and joined hands as Beth led them in prayer.

"Heavenly Father, we ask you to watch over Danny and protect him, please. We don't know where he is or why he got separated from us, but you do, and we ask you to keep him safe and help us find him quickly. Go with Jeff and the others, and give them wisdom and success in finding him. In Jesus' name, amen."

Several Mexicans and one tourist couple walking by gave the group inquisitive looks but didn't stop to ask what was going on. After wishing the search team success, the two groups parted and got back in the vans. One group headed back to San Felipe.

The other headed south toward Tulum. . . .

Turn to page 6.

We've come this far, Chris—we may as well stay with it," Willy said, sounding more confident than he felt.

Chris didn't want to be the one to wimp out either, so he swallowed hard and said, "OK, let's go."

Pushing the door open slowly, they looked and listened for any sign of the men. Seeing nothing, they ventured cautiously into the opening behind the door. Their eyes had grown accustomed to the night outside, but inside El Castillo it was pitch black. Willy, in front, put his hands out ahead of himself and strained to feel his way in. Only a few feet inside the door, he hit something with his foot. Reaching down, he discovered steps. It reminded him of the time they discovered the secret underground passages in the "ancient" Capitol Community Church back home.

"Careful, Chris," he whispered. "There are steps right in front of us."

A noise caused him to turn his head to the right, even though he couldn't see anything. Listening hard, he carefully climbed the first couple of steps—and then he saw a light.

Twenty feet farther up the stairs, the men had switched on their flashlights. They were shining their lights freely in front of them and talking in normal tones. The boys couldn't understand them, but they knew the men were speaking Spanish.

Their lack of caution now worked to Chris and Willy's advantage. Keeping a safe distance behind, the two boys crept slowly up the stairway behind the men. It was surprisingly hot and humid inside the passage, which was very narrow. Chris and Willy both hoped they wouldn't have to try to make a fast getaway down its cramped opening. The lights up ahead of them disappeared from view, but they could still see the glow they gave off.

Coming now to what they could see was the top of the stairway, the boys flattened down against the steps and peeked over the top. Ahead of them was a chamber of some kind, just as Willy had guessed. It was chained off and clearly not meant to be entered. The chamber held a number of priceless Mayan artifacts.

Willy and Chris stayed pressed against the top steps, watching as one man held out a duffel bag and the other carefully put the items into it. It was at that moment that Chris's left foot slipped off the step it was pressing against, making just enough noise to cause both men to turn and stare in their direction. The one loading the artifacts grabbed his flashlight and pointed it directly into two pairs of frightened, rounded eyes.

"Run, Willy!" Chris yelled, but he didn't need to. Willy was already three steps ahead of him down the tiny passageway. They both flew down the steps in the darkness, somehow managing to stay on their feet until they hit the wall at the bottom. Bouncing off of it, they both lunged to the left, grabbed the door, and hit the ground running outside El Castillo.

They didn't run far, though. They had barely straightened up to make their break when they ran straight into four uniformed men holding long flashlights and guns. Two were security guards, and the other two were Mexican police.

"Alto!" ("Stop!") the men yelled at Chris and Willy.

"S-s-sí, señores," Willy replied, shakily. He and Chris raised their hands without being told to.

Willy had barely gotten the words out of his mouth when the two bandits came barreling out of the pyramid. Their expressions changed from anger and annoyance to shock when they looked up into the faces—and pistols—of the four officers. They set the duffel bag down and slowly raised their own hands.

The next couple of minutes consisted of confusion interspersed with chaos, as the officers spat out questions that Chris and Willy didn't understand and the other two men didn't want to answer. In spite of the fact that they knew they wouldn't be understood, the boys tried to explain in loud, simple words and exaggerated gestures what had happened. The thieves, for their parts, rattled off rapid-fire Spanish at the officers and pointed at Chris and Willy.

Jeff arrived with Sam and Gonzo, who were able to translate back and forth between the officers and Chris and Willy. Although the officers were clearly annoyed with the boys for what they had done, they were also grateful for their help in nailing the two thieves.

88

Jeff and Matt did take Chris and Willy aside and had a long, intense talk with them about what they had done. But instead of sending them home, Jeff agreed that they could perform some "community service" back at the dorm and also for the clinic, and let it go at that. "But guys," Jeff added, "don't *ever* pull another stunt like that on me again. *Or else.*" He didn't specify what "or else" meant, and Chris and Willy didn't ask. Jeff walked away, mumbling something about "not getting paid enough for this kind of work."

THE END

For a different turn of events, turn back to page 23 or ahead to page 92.

Or, for more of *The Mayan Mystery*, turn to page 122.

Before the rest of the gang could react to what had happened, Sam took off like a shot. They heard a loud "Hey, Gonzo!" from Sam as he went around the corner after his bag.

Willy, Jessica, and Chris didn't wait long.

"Come on!" yelled Chris as he dropped his bag.

"Tallyho!" shouted Willy, peeling off the shoulder strap from his duffel.

Leaving their stuff with the others, they rushed after Sam and his friend Gonzo.

The next moments were a mass of confusion. As they rounded the corner at top speed, they came face to face with a completely unexpected scene.

Sam pursued a younger boy, who was running fast but being slowed by a large, orange duffel bag—Sam's bag.

But the boy was not Gonzo—Gonzo was right there. They all watched in shock as, unexpectedly, the young boy doubled back and Sam went right by him. Now the boy was running back toward Sam's friends, but he was looking over his shoulder at Sam. Chris and Willy stepped in front of him, and he ran into them, knocking all three of them down.

"*Qué—?*" the boy said in surprise as he struggled to free himself. But Willy held his legs and Chris held his arms until Sam arrived, out of breath.

"How come you're breathing so hard?" asked Willy with a smile. "We're the ones who caught him!"

Sam looked at Willy and then began laughing because the prisoner was still struggling and tossing Chris and Willy back and forth. *"Calma, amigo,"* ("Easy, friend") he said in a soft voice to the boy. The boy stopped immediately, shocked at hearing Sam speak to him in his own language. *"Cómo te llamas?"* ("What's your name?")

"Rodrigo," he said quietly, as if realizing that his struggles weren't going to make the two boys holding him let go. But to his amazement, as soon as he stopped struggling, Willy and Chris released him.

Just then, Jeff and one of the soldiers came hurrying around the corner. Before anyone could say a word, the soldier grabbed the young boy roughly by the shoulder and said to Jeff in broken English, "We take care of this one, señor. He was a big trouble to us." He turned with the boy and began to walk away, partly dragging his prisoner.

As the soldier was leaving, Sam called to him to wait. He and the soldier began to speak rapidly in Spanish, and the rest were left wondering what was going on.

"Sam, what are you telling him?" Jeff asked with concern in his voice.

Sam interrupted his rapid conversation with the soldier. "I'm trying to talk him into letting us take this kid and keep him with us."

CHOICE

Is it a good idea for Sam to convince the soldier to let the Ringers handle the young thief? If Jeff stops Sam from trying to convince the soldier, turn to page 34.

If the soldier just takes the boy away, turn to page 59.

No way!" Chris said, louder than he meant to. He loved adventure, too, but this was too risky. They had no idea what the two men might be up to, and nobody else would even know where they were. "Who knows what those guys are doing!"

Willy froze, torn between his curiosity and the obvious sense of what Chris was saying. Finally—and for once—caution overruled.

"Yeah, I guess you're right," Willy heard himself saying. "Let's go back and watch the rest of the show."

They rejoined the group and forgot all about the two men. That is, they forgot about them until a few weeks after they had gotten home when Willy's mother told him about an article she had read in the newspaper. The article had caught her eye because it had been written from Mérida, and since the group had just been there, Mrs. Washington read it to see if it would be of interest to Willy. The article told of a theft that had taken place at Chichén Itzá. Thieves had stolen some valuable artifacts from some of the ruins.

Authorities weren't absolutely sure when the crime had occurred, but the time frame placed it at or around the time when the group had paid their visit to the place. Upon hearing this, Willy's mouth dropped open in shock.

"Mom! Chris and I saw those guys! It was at the sound-and-light show!"

Mrs. Washington made Willy back up and tell her the whole story. As soon as he had, he picked up the phone and called Chris.

Chris couldn't believe it either. "Man, just think, Willy—we might have gotten right in the middle of a major crime. Aren't you glad we didn't follow those dudes?"

"I don't know, Chris," Willy replied. "Maybe we should have followed them and tried to stop them. Maybe we could have at least told the police what the guys looked like."

"Yeah, and maybe we could have been killed and our bodies thrown in the Well of Sacrifice, too," Chris said. "Sometimes I wonder about you, Willy."

"I know, Chris. I know it would have been dangerous," Willy went on. "But having been to Chichén Itzá, and seeing how incredible it is, I just hate hearing how those guys went and vandalized it. I just wish we could have done something, that's all."

THE END

For a different turn of events, turn to page 23.

Most people called Danny a rebel. He thought of the last words his mother had said as he left the house—*"Hope you make some friends, son"*—and then he could almost hear another voice in the back of his mind saying, *If you get friendly with these guys, your mom was right: You needed this trip.* For Danny, it was almost impossible to think that his mom could be right about anything. He knew Chris and Willy were just trying to be friendly; but down deep, he also knew that he really needed some friends.

Danny was actually very lonely. His dad had left when he was young, and he had always blamed his mother, even though she loved him and took care of him. In fact, the harder Danny's mom tried, for some reason it made him think she must be hiding something she did wrong a long time ago. But sometimes he knew that most of his problems were inside himself—and that really bothered him.

Danny thought about all this in a flash while Chris and Willy were waiting for his answer. Inside, he wanted to say, "Yeah, it would be great to room with you guys!" but instead he heard himself say, "No, I would rather stay by myself." And before the other two boys could do or say anything, Danny walked out.

CHOICE ➤➤

If Chris and Willy go after him, turn to page 137.

If Chris and Willy drop the issue for now, turn to page 69.

Willy took off his gloves, handed his shovel to Sam, and—

"No way!" he said, looking around at all the people who wanted to see him do it. "It's not worth it for twenty bucks. Besides, what am I going to do with twenty dollars here in Mexico? I've already got more pesos than I'll probably get to spend."

"Hey, Matt, I've got an idea," said Gonzalo. "Since Willy doesn't want to do it for twenty dollars, how 'bout if I throw him in, and we each get ten dollars?" With that, Gonzo grabbed Willy from behind.

"Sounds good to me," Matt answered.

Willy turned away from Gonzo, hoping to break away and run for it. Before he could move, however, Sam and Chris came up, grabbed his wrists, and the three of them swung Willy off his feet. With Chris and Sam holding his wrists and Gonzo holding his ankles, they swung Willy, screaming all the while, over the concrete pit.

"ONE . . . TWO . . . THREE!" they yelled in unison as they swung Willy over the concrete. At the last second, they yanked him back and dropped him unceremoniously on the ground beside it.

"Just kidding, dude," said Gonzo, laughing. "We wouldn't do that to you . . . unless we *each* got twenty bucks."

"Thanks a lot, you guys." Willy mocked. But he was laughing—now that he wasn't covered in concrete. "With friends like you . . ."

Finally, Saturday arrived, the last work day. All that remained to do was painting and some other finishing touches. As incredible as it seemed to them, the group had really done what they had set out to do: construct a new meeting place for the church in San Felipe. In just two short weeks—minus a couple of days off—they had built a solid, functional building that the Christians in this village would use for many purposes: worship services, educational classes, an occasional medical clinic, and more. Of course, they had had some help from some of the local people in doing some of the more skilled tasks, like stuccoing and building the roof trusses. But that just made the project all the more meaningful to them—working together with Christians from a different culture, united in their faith and their common purpose.

To the American kids, it looked like a simple, bare, concrete-block building, nothing much compared with their church facilities back home. But to Pastor Julio and his congregation, it meant everything.

"Well, Bob, what do you think?" asked Jeff. Jeff, Bob, and several of the others were standing back in the road, looking at the new building, admiring their work. "I know you kept saying we'd get it done, but are you surprised at all that we really did it?"

"No, not really," Bob answered in his slow, thoughtful way. "I knew if we hung with it we should be able to finish it. And we didn't lose too many people to sickness or dehydration. There were a couple of times I was ready to drop one or two of the kids into one of the columns and concrete 'em in, but that's about par for the course." He chuckled as he spoke.

With the prospect of getting the rest of the day off in their minds, the kids worked with renewed energy and enthusiasm. They also managed to get as much paint on each other as the walls, but nobody really minded. By 11:30 they were ready to clean up the paintbrushes and other tools and head to the market or the nearby beach.

Pastor Julio came walking over to Jeff as he was helping clean some of the brushes. Through Sam, he told Jeff of a special need that he had just become aware of and had been spending the morning looking into.

"Brother Jeff, there is a young widow with three children living in a small, run-down hut on the east side of San Felipe. Her husband died some time ago, leaving her to care for her children. She has no family in the area. Her home is badly in need of repair, and she has no money for it and no one to do it for her. I was wondering, Jeff—we have enough wood left over from our building here. Do you think some of your young people would be willing to go along with me and a couple of our men and put up a new home for her this afternoon? It could be done in one afternoon—if people are willing to work hard. What do you think?"

Jeff thought for a moment, adjusting his glasses on his nose. "Let me see if anyone would be willing, Pastor," he replied.

Bob spoke to Jeff before he could call the group together. "I'll be glad to go and supervise the project, Jeff. I don't really need anything else to take back to my family, and if we could help this lady, it would be a terrific way to end the trip."

"Thanks, Mr. Gentile," Jeff said. Calling the group together, he told them of Julio's idea. Chris, Willy, Jess, Cheryl, Sam, Gonzalo, and Carlos were all standing together. They looked at each other, all thinking the same thing: *Should we volunteer?*

If they volunteer to go, turn to page 44.

If they decide against it, turn to page 114.

We need to be committed to doing what we came here to do," Jeff said again firmly. "After we get to the work site, we can see what can be done for Rodrigo."

Sam finally got the picture. "OK."

"I'm glad you're on my side!" said Jeff as they piled their duffels and handbags into the waiting vans. "We'll have a planning meeting as soon as possible to figure how to help Rodrigo."

"Listen up, everyone!" Jeff called as he and another guy came out of the mission headquarters in Mérida. The rest of the group was loitering in the shade of the palm trees to get a break from the hot vans. "This is Dave Metzler, the short-term project director for this area. We've had a change of plans, and we're going to have to be flexible. It looks like we won't be going to San Felipe after all. I've asked Dave to tell you about it."

Dave was not a whole lot older than some of the kids—probably college age, they thought—so they wondered how he got to be a . . . "whatever-it-was" director. Although he wasn't Hispanic, they had assumed he was a native because he dressed like a Mexican. But when he started talking, it was obvious from the lack of an accent that he was from America. The Ringers listened closely.

Dave explained to the group that in a third-world

country, as in America, unexpected things often happen. "But here, it's not always a simple matter to take care of those things, and so sometimes we just have to completely change our plans." He paused, seeing the anxiety and disappointment on the kids' faces. "But don't let it get to you. One of the things you'll learn while you're here is how much God is really in control." As he talked to them about their new project, the Ringers were impressed with his maturity and his attitude toward serving God.

The vans once again started across town. Some of the other kids were grumbling about not going to San Felipe like they had planned. "Listen, guys," Jeff said. "I know it's hard to have all our plans totally change like this. But let's remember that we came here to help people and to serve God, not ourselves. Sometimes God uses things like this to teach us."

Soon the vans pulled up in front of the school building that would be home for the group during their newly assigned two-week project.

The Ringers and the others all streamed out of the vans. As Sam was about to enter the school, he happened to glance to his left. There, parked in the street in front of the next building, was a Jeep. Then he noticed, hanging over the doorway, a sign that read *Policia*.

"Unbelievable!" he practically shouted. He instantly had everyone's attention. But he didn't notice. Once again he had dropped his bag at Willy's feet and was headed toward that police station.

Sure enough, on his way into the building, he ran into

the soldier from the airport coming out to return to his post. They greeted each other with a chuckle.

Inside, Sam discovered that Rodrigo would be kept for three or four days until they could send him to a farm for orphans outside of town. In the meantime, the officer in charge gave Sam permission to visit the boy once each day. So, each evening, while others were unwinding from their hard day's work, Sam and usually one other team member would visit with Rodrigo for a while.

Willy had a hard time with the boy's name and ended up calling him "Road digger." The nickname stuck, and the little boy loved the attention.

Several times Sam explained that he wasn't angry at Rodrigo for trying to steal his bag and that he had forgiven him. He also told the boy that he could forgive because God had forgiven him, too. The idea of God's forgiveness was interesting to the little boy, who was quite a thinker.

"He's like a little brother to me," said Sam more than once. He gave Rodrigo his address at home and made the boy promise to get help to at least send Sam his address.

Sam had many adventures on this trip, but the first person he met was the one he always remembered.

THE END

Make sure you check out all the choices in this adventure. The Ringers have a chance to help many people. And they help themselves along the way, too!

By this time all the others were aware of Jess's arrival and had stopped what they were doing to stare. Beth managed to turn her around and walked away from the others with her arm around Jess's shoulders.

"It's OK, Jessica, just tell me what happened." By this time they had reached the other side of Pastor Julio's house and were out of sight of the others. Between sobs, Jess told Beth about the baby.

"Wait here, Jess," Beth said. "I want you to tell Mrs. Jordan about this." Beth left and was back in moments.

Jess told her story to Mrs. Jordan, the nurse. "It's so horrible, Mrs. Jordan! That poor woman's baby is just going to lie there until he dies!"

"Jessica, could you find the hut again? I'd like to go take a look at the baby myself. Do you think you can do it?" Mrs. Jordan's tone was kind and reassuring, but there was a tone of urgency in her words.

"Yeah, I think so." Summoning her courage, she got to her feet and led Mrs. Jordan and Beth back to the hut. Carlos and Chris were standing outside, still talking with the poor mother.

"Carlos, tell this woman that I am a nurse, and ask her if I could please see her child, will you?" Carlos turned and repeated Mrs. Jordan's words in Spanish. The woman simply nodded and walked back inside, her face drained of emotion. Mrs. Jordan followed her inside with Beth and Carlos behind her. Chris stayed outside with Jess.

After a quick examination of the almost lifeless child, Mrs. Jordan asked the mother a few questions through Carlos. Then she became very official, "Tell her I'd like to take the baby back into Mérida right now and take him to the nearest clinic. Tell her she can come along, too. I don't know if we can still help this little boy, but I sure want to try. OK?"

Once again Carlos quickly repeated her words. The mother seemed to hesitate, looking from her baby to Mrs. Jordan and back. Then she spoke to Carlos.

"She wants to know if she can go and tell her husband first," Carlos said. "She says her husband has already told her this baby is going to die, so there is no use doing anything to prolong its life."

"Tell her that he is definitely going to die if we don't get him someplace and rehydrate him. I don't know if we can still save him, but the only chance he's got is getting him to a clinic in Mérida."

Once again Carlos translated and got an answer from the woman.

"She says she has no money for a doctor."

"No money!"

Taking the woman gently but firmly by the hands, Mrs. Jordan looked into her eyes and pleaded. *"Por favor!"* It was all the Spanish she knew, but it was enough. The woman handed the baby to the nurse, grabbed a couple of personal items, and followed the others out of the hut. They went quickly back to the work site and explained the situation to Jeff and Pastor Julio. Jeff threw the keys to Matt and loaded mother, child, Pastor Julio, Mrs. Jordan, Jess, Chris, Carlos, and Beth into the van.

"Be careful, Matt!" Jeff called out as they pulled away from the site. Jeff called the rest of the team together, and they prayed for the baby. The van made the hundred-plus-mile trip to the clinic in record time.

Carlos and Julio helped the woman, señora Garcia, and her child, Miguel, out of the van and followed Mrs. Jordan into the clinic. It was a clinic run by Dr. Vargas, a Christian doctor Pastor Julio knew. Jess, Chris, Matt, and Beth came in behind them.

Julio began explaining the situation to Dr. Vargas's nurse. Sadly, she had seen hundreds of children suffering from dehydration. Some recovered, some didn't. She needed no further explanation. She motioned for the mother, baby, Julio, and Mrs. Jordan to follow her into an examining room.

As the others walked through the door leading to the examining room, Matt, Beth, Jess, Chris, and Carlos sat in the waiting room. They all felt a mixture of hope and anxiety.

"Let's pray for little Miguel," Matt said.

The five of them prayed for several minutes, asking God to heal Miguel. Just as they finished, the others came out of the back room, led by Pastor Julio.

Mrs. Jordan spoke. "The doctor has given him a nasal-gastric tube, and we're hoping we can rehydrate him. We won't know for several hours. Even then, this baby may be sick for days. I'll stay here with señora Garcia; the rest of

106

you may as well go back to San Felipe. Keep all of us in your prayers."

THE END

That's exactly what the kids did. They didn't find out how things were with little Miguel until the last day. For that story, turn to page 16.

▌ don't think that's such a good idea, Willy," Chris slowly answered. "You and I won't get much chance to talk about stuff if Danny's here in the room all the time. Besides, he probably wants his own room anyway—he sure seems to like to keep to himself. Let's just try to make it a point to talk to him while we're working or hanging out back here, OK?"

"Yeah, I guess you're right," Willy responded. He did think inviting Danny in would be the right thing to do—what Jesus would do—but he also had misgivings about Danny.

As Willy went back to unpacking his stuff, he promised himself he would look for opportunities to be a friend to Danny whenever he could.

THE END

To discover what might have happened to Danny on the trip, go back to the beginning and make different choices along the way.

At the end of a week of long, hot, exhausting days of construction work, the group was more than ready for Sunday to arrive. The plan for the day was as follows: wake-up at 7:30 A.M. instead of the usual 6:00, which drew enthusiastic support from the troops; breakfast; devotions; worship at a local church; and then off to the ancient Mayan city of Chichén Itzá for the rest of the day.

Devotions, or "E-Time," took a slightly different course for that day. After reading from one of the Psalms, Jeff asked the group to tell everyone else what this first week in the Yucatán had taught them.

Willy broke the ice. "I'm thankful I don't have to eat peanut-butter-and-mango-slime sandwiches when I get home!" This evoked howls of laughter and agreement.

"I've learned that I am unbelievably fortunate to live where I live and have all the things I have," said Cheryl. "I mean, we can all laugh about the food and the bathrooms and stuff, but that's because in another week, we're going back to the U.S., where we have all those things. What if we really lived in a place like San Felipe and that was all we would ever have or ever know? I know this, Jeff: When I get back home, I'm not going to take all that stuff for granted. I'm going to appreciate my house and our cars and going to McDonald's and everything. I'm going to be a lot more thankful for all the things God has given me."

Chris spoke up next. "God has shown me something this week, too. I've always thought that being an American Christian meant you were the best Christian in the world. You know, we can go to church without anybody throwing you in jail and all that. I always figured that because we have more open opportunities to learn about Jesus and the Bible, we must be the strongest Christians in the world. But these Yucatán Christians are *cool!*"

When Sam translated this for Pastor Julio, he and Carlos laughed out loud.

A handful of the other kids made similar comments, then Matt led them in a closing song. And Jess prayed at the end—even though it wasn't something she would normally do.

After church they drove to Mérida and ate lunch at a nice restaurant. Sitting down in a restaurant, being served by very polite waiters and waitresses, was a far cry from eating their sandwiches in the heat at the work site in San Felipe. After lunch they loaded the vans and began the hour-long drive to Chichén Itzá.

Nothing prepared them for the overwhelming experience of walking through the entrance and onto the plain of Chichén Itzá, one of the great cities of the ancient Maya. The great pyramid El Castillo towered over the area, an imposing structure that dwarfed anything they had seen on their earlier trip to Tulum. Beyond it and to the left stood the Temple of the Warriors, its hundreds of columns pointing skyward.

The group spent the afternoon looking at, climbing on, and taking pictures of the magnificent ancient city. They explored all the open buildings, feeling like a gang of young Indiana Joneses. The guys played "air football" in the old ball court, amazed at the excellent acoustics. Chris ran to one end and told Willy to whisper something to him from the other end about fifty yards away.

"You're ugly, and your mama dresses you funny," whispered Willy.

"She does not!" Chris yelled back, to the others' astonishment.

But without a doubt the highlight was climbing to the top of the great pyramid on its ninety-one stone steps. Standing on top of Castillo, looking out from each of its four sides, gave a spectacular view of the entire ruin site. The kids could not get over how a civilization that collapsed in the 1200s could have been so advanced in astronomy, mathematics, and measuring time.

The afternoon passed very quickly. As planned, the group all reassembled at the entrance at closing time. Jeff had told them to be sure to be back on time since they had made a reservation at a nearby restaurant.

As the kids all came filing in, Jeff was studying a brochure and talking with the other leaders, Matt, Bob, and Beth. "Hey, everybody, let me give you an option," he said. "There's a sound-and-light show here tonight that tells you the history of Chichén Itzá and a lot about the Maya. If you want to, we can go eat dinner, come back here at eight o'clock, catch the show, and then drive back. I know that will make for kind of a late night, but I guess we could cut you a little slack on wake-up time in the morning. What do you think?"

If the group decides to come back for the show, turn to page 133.

If the group decides *not* to come back, turn to page 116.

Chris and Willy walked out of the meeting room and into the dark.

"Tell me anything important right now, because when I slide into that sleeping bag, I'm outta here!" whipsered Willy with a yawn.

That triggered a yawn in Chris. "Whatever I have to say can wait till *mañana* [tomorrow]."

"You would have to bring up *mañana*, wouldn't you?" said Willy in mock irritation. "Next thing, you'll be reminding me to brush my teeth."

"If we keep this up, we'll never get to bed!" said Chris, running for their room.

Within a few moments, the noise quieted down in the school building. The crickets in the courtyard seemed to be the only ones awake.

Hours later there was a slight rustling sound, and a shadow moved very slowly along the porch in front of the boys' rooms.

Willy suddenly found himself wide awake. He couldn't tell how long he had been sleeping, but he was sure he had heard something.

"Did you hear that?" he whispered to Chris.

Chris only rolled over. Willy waited, hardly daring to breathe. Everything was very still and quiet. Sleep was sneaking up and had almost tackled him again when—there it was, a soft, rustling sound like someone moving outside their room. Willy shivered uncontrollably. What should he do?

If he decides to wake up Chris and check it out, turn to page 128.

If he decides to go back to sleep, turn to page 29.

The six American kids and Carlos talked among themselves. Some of them felt that they should go; others thought they were entitled to the afternoon off.

"I don't know, guys," Cheryl was saying. "I wouldn't mind helping out if we had a couple more days, but this afternoon is the last chance we'll have to goof off at the beach—and go to market. Besides, I still haven't gotten anything to take back to my family. If I go home without getting them anything from Mexico, they'll disown me."

"But don't you think helping this woman is more important?" Willy said. "I mean, I want to do some shopping, too, but how does that compare with helping put up a new house for this lady and her kids?"

"Well, look," Cheryl replied, "it's not like we're the only ones who could do this. There are twenty other people in our group who could help. And if none of us do it, you know these local men could help out, and they all know more about building than any of us except Bob. You see how fast they do stuff it takes us all day to do. I say we give her the materials and let them put the house up for her."

That seemed to satisfy the others, so none of them volunteered to go to the woman's house. Several of the other kids did, so Willy, Chris, Sam, Gonzo, Cheryl, Jess, and Carlos all went to to enjoy their afternoon off. And they did have a good time—seeing the beautiful beach, bargaining with the local merchants over handmade goods, and generally relaxing.

But in the back of their minds, they wondered. Chris especially had second thoughts, since he fancied himself the lead Ringer.

"Willy," he said that night to his buddy as they were climbing into their bunks, "we made a poor choice today, didn't we? I mean, I wanted to go to the beach and have a good time this afternoon just like everybody else. But I wonder what Jesus would have done in my place. I'm not so sure he would've gone to play or to buy T-shirts. You know what I mean?"

Willy thought for a moment and then replied, "Yeah, I know what you mean."

They said nothing more as they drifted off to sleep in the warm, humid, Yucatán night.

THE END

For a different ending to the woman's situation, turn to page 44.

The group stood there for a couple of minutes, weighing their options. Jessica, the budding historian, wanted to see the show and hear about the history of this fascinating civilization. Cheryl agreed, as did Willy and several of the others.

Sam, on the other hand, had seen all the ancient stone structures he wanted to see. Gonzo agreed with him. Being Mexican, learning more about the Maya didn't seem nearly as exotic and romantic to them as it did to Jessica. Besides, it had been a long, hot day, and they were tired. The only other adventure they wanted to tackle that day was choosing something off the menu in the restaurant.

After a few more minutes, Sam and Gonzo's appeal to the group's empty stomachs, dry throats, and tired feet won out. They elected not to return for the sound-and-light show. "We'll let Jess read to us from her tourist guidebook by flashlight on the way home," Gonzo said cheerfully. "That will be our sound-and-light show."

"Very funny," Jessica answered frostily. She was very disappointed to miss out on the opportunity to learn more about the Maya.

"OK then, troops, let's get to the restaurant," Jeff said. "I understand they have the best peanut-butter-and-mango-slime sandwiches in all of Mexico."

Like the other restaurant where they had eaten lunch,

this place was quite a step up from what they had been eating all week. The servers were used to waiting on thirsty tourists who had spent the day in the sun at Chichén Itzá, so they kept the glasses full of the cold water—purified, of course!—and whatever soft drinks the kids ordered. The food was good, too—not nearly as spicy as they expected.

It was the lack of spiciness that tempted Chris to fall for Sam's latest challenge.

"Chris?" Sam said casually.

"Yeah."

"You're a wimpy gringo, and you can't handle *real* Mexican food."

"I can eat anything you can, Sam," Chris retorted, taking the bait.

"OK, gringo," Sam said, "let's see." He called the waiter over and asked him to bring a dish of various kinds of peppers along with a basket of tortilla chips. When the items arrived, Sam pushed them in front of Chris and said, "Dig in—if you think you're man enough."

"I said I'd eat anything you did," Chris replied. "You start, and I'll finish. We'll see who expires first."

"OK, gringo," Sam said, a mischievous twinkle in his eye. "Just one more thing. No water or anything else to drink. The first one that reaches for his glass is 'el wimpo.'"

By now everyone had gathered around to watch this contest of fools. Sam took a chip, scooped up a green pepper, and ate it. "Delicious," he declared.

Chris did the same, selecting the same kind of pepper as Sam. "Child's play," he said as he swallowed.

Sam took another; so did Chris. Each time, the boys

tried their hardest to make it seem as if there was nothing to it. Each time, it got a little harder.

After the sixth round, both boys had sweat glistening on their foreheads.

After the ninth, Chris's nose was running. His mouth was on fire. He tried not to show it, but he was clearly in pain and dying to reach for his water glass.

Sam was hurting, too, but doing a better job of covering it up. Although he was born and raised in the U.S., his family did occasionally eat more traditional Mexican-style food, and Sam's father loved jalapeños and other kinds of hot peppers. Sam had therefore developed more of a tolerance for them, and he was counting heavily on it.

By the time Sam put the eleventh pepper in his mouth, Chris, still trying to act cool and composed, had tears in his eyes. He watched as Sam chewed up the little instrument of torture, smiled, and said with a numb tongue, "Your turn, gringo."

Chris picked up a chip and started to reach for the peppers. The thought of putting one more into his already burning mouth was more than he could stand. He wavered for a second, dropped the chip, and lunged for his glass of water. He had lost, but at that moment all he cared about was putting out the fire.

"YES!" Sam cried. "I told you you would be 'el wimpo.'" He smiled, enjoying his triumph. He, too, however, was feeling the burn of all those peppers, and so he didn't gloat too long. After Chris had guzzled down his glass, Sam reached for his . . . only to see Gonzo snatch it away from him at the last second.

Sam looked around for another glass, realizing to his horror that they had all been removed. There was not a drop of liquid in sight.

"Who's 'el wimpo' now, gringo?" Gonzo said, holding Sam's water glass away from him. "You won the battle, but I think you will lose the war!"

Sam lunged for the glass, to the amusement of everyone else in the group, especially Chris. "Have another pepper, *hombre*," he called.

Realizing he would get no sympathy—and no liquid—from his buddies, Sam made a beeline for the kitchen. He knew he could talk *someone* into giving him a drink. He did, too, but not before everyone had a good laugh on him. Even after several glasses, he and Chris both felt the aftereffects of their ill-advised contest.

"Never again," Chris promised.

"Boys!" said Jess.

THE END

What other adventures await the group at the Mayan ruins? To find out, turn back to page 108 and make different choices.

Willy spoke up first. "Come on, Chris. Let's go do it and see the rest of the village."

Chris thought for a moment, then nodded his agreement. Beth began to instruct the "mission team" in what to say. Mainly she needed to tell Carlos and Sam because they would be doing all the talking. It only took a couple of minutes, since the kids were going to simply spread the word that Bible school for the local children would be held every afternoon just after lunch. It would meet at one of the few open, shaded areas in the village, just a block away from the construction site. Concluding the instructions, Beth smiled and said, "Have fun! And be back by lunchtime, OK?"

"No problem there!" said Willy, smiling.

Chris and Jessica agreed to go with Carlos, while Willy, Cheryl, Gonzo, and Sam teamed up into a second group. "Let's go, gringos," Sam called with mock disgust. After conferring briefly with Carlos—or "Charlie," as they had begun to call him—about the layout of the village, the two teams split up. There wasn't that much to San Felipe, so the directions didn't take long. Carlos's group headed east from the work site; Sam and Gonzo's group went west.

To travel with Carlos's group, turn to page 20.
To travel with Sam and Gonzo's group, turn to page 49.

Chris thought for a minute, then said, "Nah—he's either back at the *baño* or talking with somebody back there by the entrance. He's probably seen this show before and just didn't feel like sitting through it again."

That satisfied Willy, so the two of them sat with the rest of the group. The narrator with the heavy Mexican accent told the legend of where the Maya came from and how they had settled Chichén Itzá. The group learned a great deal more about the buildings and the artwork they had been climbing on all day: The Nunnery, so named because it reminded an early Spanish writer of the Catholic nunneries in Spain; the Caracol, an ancient astronomical observatory; the Ball Court, where warriors played a game that had high stakes—the winning team's captain beheaded the losing team's; the Temple of the Warriors and the Thousand Columns, once the most beautiful structure in all of Chichén Itzá; and much more. But the highlight of the evening was the story of El Castillo, the great pyramid, known to the Maya as the Temple of Kukulcán.

According to legend, Kukulcán was a great statesman and ruler who had led a group of people from the central part of Mexico to found the city of Chichén Itzá somewhere around the year A.D. 987. He was known as Quetzalcóatl by the Aztecs, a name that means "feathered serpent." The temple of Kukulcán was built in his honor and stands today as the most spectacular structure in all the Yucatán.

Great care went into the building of the great pyramid. Each side has a total of 91 steps leading to the top, adding up to 364; one more step at the top, leading into the temple itself, makes 365—the number of days in the year. Each year at the two equinoxes—the beginning of spring and the beginning of fall—the sun rises and shines on the pyramid in such a way as to make the shadows look like a great serpent gliding down the side.

"That would be so cool to see," Jess whispered to Cheryl.

"The great Kukulcán," the narrator continued, "having settled Chichén Itzá and governed it wisely for many years, also taught his people the way of virtue. Some loved him for his wisdom, but many others resented him for his goodness and refused to try to live as he taught them. Saddened by their foolishness, Kukulcán left the people, departing to the east from the coast of Yucatán. He said that one day, when men were wiser and more ready to receive his teachings, he would return the same way he left. We, the descendants of the Maya, long for that day. . . ."

Just as he finished speaking, the temple on top of the pyramid was filled with brilliant light. Everyone oohed and aahed again, thinking they had saved the best for last. But one more surprise remained.

As everyone's eyes were focused on the top of El Castillo, a figure emerged on top of the lighted building. He was wearing a serpent mask and a long headdress of beautiful feathers. He raised his arms toward the audience,

124

and, to their delight, there was a flash of light and a rush of dense smoke at the figure's feet. He spread his feathered arms, leaped from the edge of the temple, and disappeared!

The whole crowd gasped and jumped to its feet, applauding the terrific show and spectacular ending. As they continued to cheer, however, Chris looked at Willy, and Willy returned his glance.

"Are you thinking what I'm thinking, bro?" Chris asked.

"Absolutely," replied Willy.

"Then let's go!"

CHOICE

Turn to page 65.

There's gotta be *something* we can do, Jeff! *Please!*"

Jeff hesitated, obviously struggling with what to say. Finally, "I do know someone who might be able to help Rodrigo—"

Sam lit up. "Call him now!"

"—but I can't call him right now," Jeff insisted. "We've got twenty-five people involved in this trip, and we just can't follow every little rabbit trail we come to."

Sam blew up. "Rabbit trail, shmabbit trail! Don't you *care* about people? Rodrigo is obviously a little boy, and they're taking him to jail!"

Jeff tried to calm Sam down, but the younger Ringer refused to respond. He stormed off in protest, not only angry at not being able to do anything but angry at Jeff himself.

But Jeff was right. There simply was no way they could force help on Rodrigo, as much as they—or Sam, really—wanted to.

Later that week Jeff did make some phone calls in an attempt to find out what he could about Rodrigo's fate. But he tried not to give Sam any false hopes.

Jeff stopped by Sam's room for a chat. He didn't look very happy about the news he had to bring.

"I've been on the phone with some people I thought

might be able to help us with Rodrigo's problem. It doesn't look good, Sam. That boy has gotten himself in a lot of trouble. He hasn't been an orphan too long, but he's already got quite a reputation as a thief," said Jeff thoughtfully.

Sam wanted to get to the point. "What'll happen to him?" he asked.

"It already did," said Jeff. "The soldiers took him before a juvenile judge, and Rodrigo was sent to a special ranch they have for orphans up in the hills. He'll be held there while they try to find a family willing to adopt him. He's still young enough that there's a chance."

Sam stared off into space for a moment, then said very slowly, "You mean there's nothing we can do for him."

Jeff took a deep breath. "Sam, you can't just help people because you want to. You have to get permission from a lot of people and do it with respect for the ones you're reaching out to. You're an American. You feel powerful. You feel like you have a lot. Rodrigo doesn't have a lot. But that doesn't mean you can just swoop in and rescue him like Superman. You pray for the person, do what you can, and leave the rest to God."

Sam felt a tear fall down his cheek. "There's nothing we can do for him," he repeated.

"Not exactly," answered Jeff. "You will probably never see him again, but I did get permission for you to write him a letter and for us to send him some of the materials we brought down to use in the Bible school. We'll include a Spanish New Testament for him, too. Rodrigo can't read, but the judge told me someone at the ranch would be glad to read to him."

Sam immediately began going through his stuff, pulling out paper and pen. "I guess I'd better get busy!"

THE END

After the trip was over, Sam still prayed for Rodrigo once in a while and wrote often to the little orphan thief. He often wondered if Rodrigo would make it to the States for his own adventure with the Ringers. . . .

Willy crept out of bed, shook Chris awake, and whispered, "Shhhh! Someone's moving outside."

"Are you sure?" Chris asked, stifling a yawn.

"Hey! I'm not crazy, you know!" whispered Willy.

The boys slowly opened their door and stuck their heads out so they could look both ways on the porch. The moon was bright, so they could see their side of the courtyard clearly, but the opposite porch was in the shadows.

Willy motioned for them to crouch down, and they slipped across to the edge of the porch and behind a solid short wall that separated the porch from the courtyard. The wall had an opening on each side that led to a walkway among the trees.

Willy was about to lead the way to one of those openings when he caught a movement out of the corner of his eye. At the same instant, he heard the rustling sound again. He looked back toward their room and saw someone standing right by their doorway. It looked like the person was bending over to peek into their room.

Willy grabbed for Chris and pointed. To his utter surprise, Chris fell over onto the ground and began rolling with laughter. Willy leaped to his feet in confusion and found that now there were two someones by their room.

In an instant he realized his mistake. He swung

around to look at the courtyard and saw a palm tree whose branches cast a humanlike shadow on the wall of the porch. When he had stood up, his own shadow had been added to the mysterious courtyard visitor's shadow near the doorway!

Chris, still laughing, crawled back into their room on his hands and knees. Willy shook his head and returned to his own bunk. "I promise not to tell if you don't!"

Chris just chuckled.

To catch up with them the next morning, turn to page 29.

Danny had never experienced anything like the urge he felt to stand up and confess before all these people how empty his life had been, how desperately unhappy he was. He didn't know why, but he felt that he should tell them about his hurt and loneliness, ask them to pray for him, and ask them to tell him how he could be like them.

He felt the Holy Spirit urging him to speak . . . but he couldn't do it. He was too scared. Too afraid.

Danny sat silently, not moving. Though his life was a mess, at least it was familiar.

The adventure in the Yucatán ended sadly for Danny. He could have gone home a brand new person. Instead, he went back the same.

At least for now.

THE END

For a different choice for Danny and to find out what else happened at the end of the trip, turn to page 139.

Willy turned back toward the hut so fast that he almost slipped and fell. The hinge gave way when he yanked on the door, so he pushed the cracked boards out of the way and lunged into the hut, which now seemed to be alive. It was making all sorts of slurping and groaning noises.

Willy saw Danny immediately. He was right where they had left him, frozen with fear in the corner of the hut. Without saying a word, Willy grabbed Danny by his denim lapels and dragged him toward the door. Suddenly, Chris was right beside him, helping.

At first it was like dragging a sack of stones, but then Danny seemed to come out of his daze. He began to scramble with them. They were in the doorway when the noises got louder and the entire hut collapsed. The opening they had just passed through twisted into a crazy shape and then disappeared under the roof thatch and the muddy water. Willy thought later that it almost looked like a large ship sinking. Only this was a shelter they had just been inside!

They waded to the first high ground they found before they looked back. There was a mound of dirt where the hut had been, and pieces of the roof were still floating away. A shudder went through all of them.

"That was too close!" said Chris. "What happened, Danny?"

Danny looked at them both blankly, water streaming down his face. "I don't know. It was like I couldn't move. I knew I had to get out, but I was so scared my legs wouldn't work!" He looked away for a second and then added, "Thanks for coming back for me. If you hadn't, I might not even be here right now."

"No problema, amigo!" said Willy, happy that maybe things were going to work out with Danny after all.

The boys were shivering badly in the rain, though the worst of the storm had passed. They jogged back up to the work site and helped with the cleanup. Fortunately, the work crew had noticed the storm coming and had covered the work site with tarps to protect it. There was still plenty of work to do that day, and the boys figured they had had their share of fun!

THE END

Danny just might become quite a friend. If you don't yet know how, turn back to the beginning and make different choices along the way.

Let's come back and see this sound-and-light show, Jeff," Jessica volunteered. "That's something we might never get another chance to do."

After a little more discussion, Jessica's suggestion carried the day. They drove off for the restaurant, tired and hungry, but also excited about seeing the ruins at night.

The restaurant was similar to the one at lunch: traditional Mexican decorations, mariachi music playing over the speakers in the ceiling, polite, well-dressed waiters and waitresses. After the long, hot afternoon climbing around the ruins, the entire group was especially grateful for another good meal and *lots* of water and sodas.

At 7:45 Jeff announced it was time to go back to Chichén Itzá for the show. The sun was just setting as they made the short trip back to the ruins.

"This is going to be seriously cool," Jess said excitedly.

"It better be," chimed in Chris, "or we're throwing you into the Well of Sacrifice."

"Thanks for the encouragement," responded Jess.

When they got back to the ruins, there were seats lined up several rows deep near the edge of the plain. Attendance was pretty good that night. There were a number of European tourists, two families that looked like typical midwestern Americans, quite a few others of undetermined origin, and two men who sat at the very back on the near edge of the seats. Jeff and the group filled up the first two rows.

They had barely gotten seated when a taped voice greeted them in heavily accented English, "Good evening, ladies and gentlemen!"

The voice went on to explain that they were going to see and hear a presentation that would give them some insight into the story of the great city of Chichén Itzá and the history of the Mayan people. It was totally dark by now, and the kids could see the dark silhouettes of the structures against the starry sky. It was very impressive, and Jessica felt as though the ancient Maya could have materialized from the woods around them and resumed their lives right then and there.

"Yo, Willy," Chris whispered. "Where's Carlos?"

Even though Carlos didn't speak English very well, Willy and Chris had gotten to know the Mexican boy quite well and had become good friends.

"I don't know," Willy replied. "He was right behind you when we walked in. Did he say he was going to do something else?"

"He didn't tell me," Chris answered. "Maybe he just went to the *baño*."

Willy asked, "Should we go back to look for him?"

CHOICE ⇒

If Chris and Willy go to look for Carlos, turn to page 72.

If they stay put, turn to page 122.

Sam and Gonzo were caught off guard as they came around the back of the tool trailer. Jess stood there, red-faced and flustered, holding a shovel like a baseball bat.

"All right," she said, "you guys have about three seconds to tell me who or what you were whispering about back there!"

The boys looked instantly embarrassed. They glanced at each other and then discovered something very interesting to stare at on the tops of their shoes.

"We were sorta having a disagreement," Sam muttered. "Anyway, it's settled."

"No, it's *not*," Gonzo countered under his breath.

"Yes it *is*, bean brain," Sam countered under *his* breath.

"Not!" said Gonzo loudly, suddenly smiling.

Sam glared at his friend, blushing like crazy.

"Oh, I can't stand it anymore. I'll confess," said Gonzo. Before Sam could open his mouth or shut Gonzo's, Gonzo blurted out, "Sam likes somebody, but he can't tell her."

"Oh!" said Jess, lowering the shovel.

Sam put out his hand and asked, "Could I borrow that shovel? I would like to dig for buried treasure in Gonzo's head."

Jess pulled the shovel farther out of reach. "That's sweet, Sam," she said, smiling. "Who is she?"

Gonzo was about to make another contribution to the conversation when Sam clamped his hand over his mouth. "Don't . . . even . . . *think* . . . about . . . it!" Sam threatened.

The mystery of Sam's female interest never did come out in the open, but Jess wondered. It seemed to her that Sam went out of his way to be nice to her. And she began to notice him, too, and thought he was pretty neat. She thought maybe they would be better friends when they got home.

She whistled as she picked up the rest of her tools.

THE END

Sam's a great guy, but, like most boys his age, a little shy around girls. To find out some of the other adventures they all had together, make sure you try out all the possible adventures in *The Mayan Mystery!*

Chris and Willy looked at each other completely
stunned. They weren't mad at Danny for turning down
their offer, but it did hurt a little.

Willy wheeled around and chased after Danny. "Oh no
you don't," he said under his breath.

The slender boy was hunched in his denim jacket and
headed for the front door. Willy caught up with him and
walked alongside. "Hey, look, if you don't want to room
with us that's fine. Probably a good idea—did I tell you
Chris snores? He'll deny it, of course, but that's the way we
all are. You have to tape-record a snorer to make him
believe it—and sometimes even then he thinks you just
made it up. . . ." Willy was talking faster than he could
think. He stopped to take a breath.

Danny kept walking.

"Hey, man!" said Chris from somewhere behind him.
Danny froze in his tracks, thinking he was about to have a
fight on his hands. "Listen to my friend Willy, here. He's just
trying to let you know it's cool if you want to hang around
with us. You can walk away, but remember, we're on this
trip together. We may drive you crazy, but if we did, then
you'd be in good company. Do I really snore, Willy? How
come you never told me before?"

"OK! OK!" said Danny in surrender. "Thanks for
letting me stay with you, but I think I'd rather stay by

myself, at least for now. You guys want to harass me—go right ahead. It'll make my day."

Willy turned to Chris in mock surprise. "Did he really say 'make my day'? I can't believe it! Consider it done, Danny. The Ringers strike when you least suspect them!"

"Ringers?" Danny asked with a contorted expression.

Chris and Willy explained the connection to Miss Whitehead and to ringing the church bell. "A ringer is a person who's like someone else, and we're supposed to be like Jesus . . . ," began Willy.

" . . . and we ring the church bell every Sunday," added Chris.

"So we're Ringers."

"Oh," Danny said.

With that, Chris and Willy turned back to their room, and Danny stepped outside into the late afternoon shadows. He wondered what these next two weeks would be like. What *would* they be like hanging around with religious kids?

He was going to be pleasantly surprised.

THE END

For a sampling of what did happen, turn to page 108.

Or, turn to page 26 and continue the story.

Danny got up to speak. He cleared his throat, his mind racing. "I didn't know any of you when I came on this trip. I really only came because my mom *made* me come." He paused, then went on. "I thought all of you were really strange at first, talking about Jesus and being servants. I figured if that's what you want to do with your life, fine, but I wanted a lot more out of life than some stupid religious game. That's why I kept to myself and never really hung around any of you—except for Chris and Willy, and that was only because they bugged me until I said OK."

Chris and Willy smiled.

"I was thinking that I was way too cool for that, and I put you all down because you were on this religious trip, and . . . and then it hit me: There wasn't anything in my life to feel cool about. You guys weren't the ones who were settling for second best—*I* was. And that really rattled my cage.

"Well, as all the gringos know, about a week ago, I tried to do something about my messed-up life. I thought I could just run away from it. I know what I did was really stupid, and I've apologized to everybody I could. I want to say again how sorry I am and ask you all again to forgive me . . . I'm sorry. And I want to thank Jeff for giving me another chance. Thanks, man." Jeff nodded at him.

"What I'm trying to say is that what this trip has showed me is that I can't run away from my problems. It isn't *where* I am that's messing me up; it's *what* I am. We built this building so that you people could use it to do God's work, and I guess I'm the first person he needs to work on in here. Whatever it means to ask Jesus to come into my heart, I want to do that right now."

A group of the kids, led by Chris and Willy, came over to Danny. Matt, Beth, and Jeff came, too, putting their arms around him or their hands on his shoulders.

Jeff asked Matt if he would pray for Danny, and he readily agreed. While everyone else in the place prayed for him—in two languages—Matt prayed with him, and Danny became a Christian.

That dedication service was unlike anything any of the kids had ever been to before. In the months and years to come, they would all remember it as the highlight of the trip.

There were a lot of tearful good-byes that day, and a lot of promises to write letters. Most of the kids kept their promises. Carlos especially got a lot of pen pals that day and numerous offers of places to stay if he could ever come visit the States.

They flew home the next morning, tired, suntanned, and changed by their experiences in the Yucatán Peninsula. None of the people on that trip could ever look at the world or their faith in quite the same way after such an intense, powerful encounter with God's work and his people in that unfamiliar culture.

Saying good-bye to Gonzo at the Mérida airport was sad. He had to take a different flight back to Miami, and his left ninety minutes after theirs. He got lots of hugs and handshakes and promises to stay in touch.

"Hasta la vista, y'all!" he yelled as the group walked out to board their flight back to Washington. "You're not bad for a bunch of gringos!"

As for Willy, Chris, Jeff, Sam, Jessica, Cheryl, Matt, Beth, and the others, they spent the flight home talking about what a great experience it had been. Danny surprised them all by taking an active part in the conversation. He even took off his denim jacket and loaned it to Jessica when she got cold, and he didn't even ask to sit by the window.

THE END

The Ringers decided that sticking together is what they did best. Before long, they were all hauling, nailing, and lifting together.

"I just have one question," said Willy as he lifted yet another concrete block into position. "Will I ever get my fingerprints back?"

The building crew discovered rather quickly that building with concrete blocks is hard because of the weight of the blocks, not because great skill is needed. It was all the more impressive considering that none of the kids had ever done this kind of work before—mixing concrete by hand, hauling mortar in buckets, laying concrete blocks. Except for Matt, who had worked construction one summer, none of the adults had either.

By the end of the first morning, the crew had learned how to mix and apply mortar, hang a plumb line, lay a course of blocks, and many other basic skills involved in construction. Bob was an excellent and patient teacher. Instead of calling him Bob, the kids quickly decided he was Mr. Gentile, and the name stuck.

During lunch the first day Mr. Gentile said, "You kids make a great crew. I've taught you basically everything you need for this project. Now you have to do those things over and over again. But just in case you forget, I guess I'll stick around to remind you."

Jeff added, "The kind of building we are doing reminds me a lot of the life God wants us to have. There are certain skills we need to learn—like how to read the Bible and how to pray and how to talk to others about what we believe. Once we know these skills, we have to practice them over and over and over. It isn't always easy, but in the end, we will have a life like a building, complete and helpful to others."

The excitement of being on a mission trip wore off in the next couple of days as the team got going on the work they had come to do. There were jobs that no one really wanted, like hauling the water barrels around to be refilled and lifting heavy bags of cement mix. But all the kids soon realized that each of them would have to do things he or she wasn't crazy about doing, or the project would never get done.

Mr. Gentile managed to keep everybody in good spirits. "Keep cool," he would say at least a dozen times a day. "Stay loose. Have fun. We'll get this puppy finished. And if not . . . I know which ones of you I want to leave behind to finish it up for us."

One especially hot afternoon—"Hot as a big dog," as Mr. Gentile would say—several of the guys were mixing a large batch of concrete to pour columns. Standing beside the pit with a shovel in his hands, Matt looked over at Willy, who was standing on the opposite side of him. "Yo, Willy. I got twenty dollars that says you won't put your face in that batch of concrete."

Willy looked at Matt, and then at the large, wet, grayish mass of concrete before him looking like "the blob that would eat Willy Washington."

"Twenty bucks? To go face-first into that mess?" Willy thought about it. "You got the money on you right now?"

Matt took off his right glove, reached into his pocket, and pulled out a combination of American dollars and Mexican pesos. Locating a dirty twenty-dollar bill, he waved it at Willy and said, "Right here, homey. Are you man enough?"

By now everybody was watching, cheering Willy on. "Do-it! Do-it! Do-it!" Several of the others said, "If Willy won't do it, I will!"

Matt kept his eyes on Willy. "Nope," he said. "This is a onetime offer, from me to Mr. Washington. What's it going to be, homey?"

Willy took one more look at Matt's twenty dollars and then another at the pit full of concrete in front of him. Willy knew what he had to do.

CHOICE ➤

If Willy goes for it, turn to page 35.

If he turns it down, turn to page 96.

Since only a handful were needed for the children's project, the Ringers elected to work on the building. Jeff gathered that crew at one end of the room and reviewed the plans.

Their mission was to help build a small concrete block building in the village of San Felipe for a group of local Christians. The people had been meeting together as a church for several years, but since they didn't have the money to build anything, they had been meeting in a member's home. But the church had grown, and the house was now too small to hold them. For months the church services had included members sitting or standing outside in the dirt yard. They really needed a bigger building.

Then, through a series of contacts, they had hooked up with Fairfax Congregational Church, where Jeff served as youth pastor. That had led to this team of young people and a few adults coming together to work with the local Christians. They only had two weeks to accomplish the project, and it was going to be difficult work.

As Jeff finished his talk, he told the kids to get into small groups with one of the adults and spend a few minutes praying for a good attitude, good health, safety, and, most important, that they would be good witnesses for Christ. Chris, Willy, Jess, Cheryl, Sam, and Gonzo naturally huddled together and, with some persuasion, convinced

Danny to join them. Matt sat in as the adult in their group. Except for Danny, they all prayed.

As the kids were wrapping up the prayer time, they noticed that Jeff and a couple of the other adults were talking with a young Mexican boy who looked to be about the same age as the American kids. He was dark-skinned and short, with coal-black hair and chiseled facial features. His cheekbones and nose were unusual, making him look like the pictures they had seen of Native Americans.

When the last group was done praying, Jeff said, "Hey, I want you guys to meet a new friend and coworker. This is Carlos—he lives in San Felipe, and he's going to work with us in the village and spend some time with us here at the school. And best of all, he speaks some English, so he can help Samuel and Gonzo with interpreting for the rest of us."

That met with a sincere round of applause. While some of the kids had taken a Spanish class or two, it had not prepared them for the Yucatán nor for the speed at which the locals talked. They were all grateful to have another bilingual member of the team.

As the meeting broke up, the kids still had about an hour before lights-out. Some of them headed back to their bunks, some stayed in the meeting room to talk, and some went outside to goof around. Sam and Gonzo made a beeline for Carlos, eager to talk to another person who shared their Mexican heritage and spoke the same two languages.

"Willy," Chris said, "let's go over with Sam and Gonzo."

After Chris and Willy had listened to their conversation in Spanish for a few moments, Willy asked,

"Man, do you guys always talk that fast when you're talking Spanish?"

Sam and Gonzo looked at each other, shrugging their shoulders. "I didn't know we talked any faster in Spanish than in English," said Gonzo.

"It sure sounds like it," agreed Chris. "We wanted to meet Carlos and talk with him, too, but we'll probably need you guys' help."

"OK," Sam volunteered. "But Carlos probably speaks enough English that you won't need us. Right, Carlos?"

Carlos smiled and slowly said in heavily accented English, "I am not so sure that is true." Something about the way he said it made the others all laugh.

"Well, even so, you just said more in English than I can in Spanish, so we better give your English a try," Willy said. "Tell us about yourself. If you don't know how to say something, let Sam or Gonzo help you out."

For the next forty-five minutes, Carlos told the other four boys about himself and his life in the Yucatán. His mother and father had died in an epidemic when he was a child, so he knew almost nothing about his birth parents. Fortunately, an old woman who apparently had lived in the same village had taken Carlos in and cared for him for a while. But her own health wasn't good, so she brought him to Pastor Julio and his wife, Rosa. The pastor and his wife were unable to have children of their own, and they had prayed that somehow God would give them at least one child to love and to raise. When they saw baby Carlos, they knew their prayers had been answered, and they loved him and cared for him as their own son.

Once they adopted Carlos, he became known to everyone in San Felipe as "Carlos Celiz," only son of Julio and Rosa. Even so, most of the older people in the village knew his story, and they felt a special love for him, just as they did for the faithful pastor and his wife. In a sense, the whole village "adopted" him.

"Wow," said Willy. "That's quite a story. Do you know anything about your real parents, or where you came from, or any of that kind of stuff?"

"Well," Carlos replied, "Julio and Rosa are my 'real' parents, as far as I'm concerned. But no, I don't know much about my birth parents or my other family members or anything. Old señora Javier, who took me in and brought me to my parents, also died a long time ago, so I have no one to ask these kinds of things. But there is one other thing that might be of interest to you. It's about my ancestors . . . ," Carlos began to explain.

Just at that moment Jeff announced that it was fifteen minutes till lights-out and that everyone needed to get to their rooms and get ready for bed.

"*Bueno,*" Carlos said. "Another time I will finish my story."

"Cool," said Willy.

"*Gracias,* Carlos," Chris said in his best Mexican tones. "I'm glad you're going to be working with us. And I want to hear a lot more about life in the Yucatán, OK?"

"*Sí, señor,*" answered Carlos. "*Con mucho gusto.*" ("With much pleasure.")

"I understood the 'Sí, señor' part," said Chris. "But what was the rest of it?"

Sam volunteered, "Carlos said, 'Yes sir. You are a bonehead.'"

With that parting shot, the four kids from the U.S. said good night to Carlos and headed for their bunks. Carlos, smiling and shaking his head at the same time, headed outside to where his ride home was waiting. Tomorrow would come very early for all of them.

CHOICE ⇒

If Chris and Willy decide they should go right to sleep, turn to page 112.

If instead they stretch their day a little, turn to page 80.

Danny seemed to be having a hard time deciding.

"Hey, I know Willy's black, and sometimes it's hard to see him at night, but don't let that scare you." Chris had barely gotten this out of his mouth before he cracked up laughing. Less than a second later, Willy, also laughing, was shoving Chris over an empty school desk and had started whaling away at him for his remark. Both of them ended up on the ground, gasping for air.

Even Danny couldn't help but join in the laughter. "OK, you guys. It looks like you need a keeper anyway. But I'm asking Jeff for half my money back for having to put up with you." This just made Chris and Willy laugh all the harder—none of the kids had ever heard Danny say anything the least bit funny before. When they were finally under control again, they straightened up the desks they'd scattered, helped Danny with his stuff, and moved him into their room.

Later that afternoon Cheryl made a sign for their door that read The Three Amigos. Before lights-out that night, someone had scratched out *Amigos* and scribbled *Stooges*.

Turn to page 26.

Kent Keller
is Director of Christian Education and Discipleship
Ministries at Key Biscayne Presbyterian Church in Key
Biscayne, Florida. He lives in Miami with his wife Heidi
and their two children Chris and Andrew.

*If you enjoy **Choice Adventures**, you'll want to read these exciting series from Tyndale House Publishers!*

You can find Tyndale books at fine bookstores everywhere. If you are unable to find these titles at your local bookstore, you may write for ordering information to:

Tyndale House Publishers
Tyndale Family Products Dept.
Box 448
Wheaton, IL 60189